I YANK MY HAND AWAY. IT'S TOO MUCH. I CAN'T—
I can't feel this. I can't do this. I stand and flee the room
before he can finish saying my name, run out of his
house, start the long walk home with tears in my eyes.

I don't need a new person to suddenly spring up
under my skin and push out who I was, who I've already
decided to be. Those feelings have no place in my life and
I will not let myself be a fool in love, with love, let it take
over and destroy me.

Love isn't magic. Just like my family, just like my
place in the universe, it's something that I can't keep,
can't make last.

ALSO BY
KIERSTEN WHITE

ILLUSIONS OF FATE

MIND GAMES
PERFECT LIES

PARANORMALCY
SUPERNATURALLY
ENDLESSLY

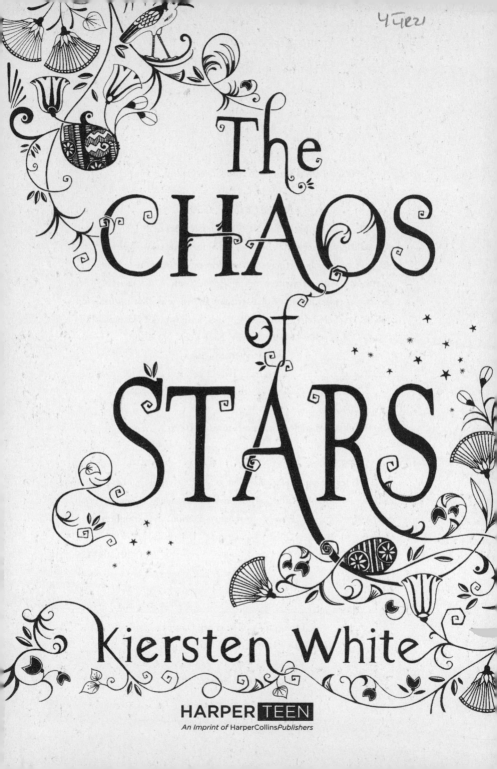

The CHAOS of STARS

Kiersten White

HARPER TEEN

An Imprint of HarperCollinsPublishers

HarperTeen is an imprint of HarperCollins Publishers.

The Chaos of Stars
Copyright © 2013 by Kiersten Brazier
www.epicreads.com

Library of Congress Cataloging-in-Publication Data
White, Kiersten.
      The chaos of stars / Kiersten White. — 1st ed.
          p.   cm.
      ISBN 978-0-06-213587-2 (pbk.)
      [1. Interpersonal relations—Fiction.   2. Mythology, Egyptian—
Fiction. 3. Gods—Fiction. 4. Goddesses—Fiction. 5. Isis (Egyptian
deity)—Fiction. 6. Family problems—Fiction. 7. Immortality—
Fiction.   8. San Diego (Calif.)—Fiction.] I. Title.
PZ7.W583764Ch   2013   2012038129
[Fic]—dc23   CIP
                                                                 AC

Typography by Torborg Davern
14 15 16 17 18   LP/RRDH   10 9 8 7 6 5 4 3 2 1

First paperback edition, 2014

For my mother, Cindy, goddess of lost keys
And my father, Patrick, god of emergency
grocery-store runs

When I was a little girl, I still believed I was part of the world's secret magic.

Mother wrapped her hair elegantly in white cloth. I begged and pleaded until she did mine as well. At the river, Mother gathered pebbles and sand, small plants, sun-bleached bones. I splashed along the banks, or rode on female hippos if Taweret, my aunt and the goddess of childbirth, was with us.

But my favorite place to be, even more than in the brilliant sun reflecting off the water of the Nile, was with my father. When I was old enough to navigate the steep, worn steps by myself, I was there every minute Mother allowed. As soon as I finished my morning worship, I'd skip straight down. Coloring on the floor next to Father's knees as he nodded and watched things I couldn't see. Giggling as I ran between Ammit's unmoving lion and hippo legs. Memorizing the pictures along the walls, making up stories for the people portrayed there.

Mother gave me my very own paints, and Father proudly gave me a room. I'd never been happier. Countless hours down there I painted, sketched, planned. I drew the stories of my life on those walls, filled them with the people and places I loved. My mom, beautiful and strong. My dad, serene and kind. Grandma Nut stretching across the sky to watch us all. They were my family; they were my story.

My cat, cranky old Ubesti, came down with me sometimes, though she much preferred the warm, sunlit stones under the skylights in our house. One morning when I was barely thirteen, I decided I needed a live model for her newest portrait on my walls. She was in her usual spot, mangy fur dull and matted even in the light. I went to pick her up, expecting a yowl of protest, but was met instead with a limp, lifeless body.

My mother immediately knew something was wrong and came into the room to find me crying. She consoled me with a hug that soothed my hiccupping sobs, and a kiss that made my head stop hurting from the tears.

"Don't worry, Little Heart," she said. "How would you like Ubesti to be yours forever?"

I nodded, desperate. I'd seen my mother heal sick locals, witnessed her save a baby others had given up for dead. She was *magic*. Surely bringing my elderly cat back from death would be no problem—after all, she'd resurrected my father. Death was not a barrier for Isis.

She took Ubesti's body from my arms and told me to meet her downstairs in my room. I nearly tripped in my haste to get there, pacing with nervous excitement. Even after all the potions and amulets I'd helped her with, she'd never done actual spells for me, and at that moment I loved her even more than I knew possible.

My father came in, smiling his soft, distant smile, and my mother followed him, beaming and carrying a large jar in her hands. It was carved with glyphs, the lid shaped like a cat's head, all made in precious alabaster.

"What's that?" I asked, eager to see what resurrection required.

"This is the vessel that will carry Ubesti to the other side, where she will wait for you." Osiris nodded solemnly as my mother handed him the jar and he placed it on the large block of stone that I used as a table in the middle of the room.

"Wait—other side? What other side?"

"The afterlife," my father said, looking at me with pride in his eyes. "I am pleased you chose her as a companion for your journey through death."

I staggered back, staring in horror at the jar I now realized contained my cat. "You—she's not coming back to life?"

"No, Little Heart, not to this life."

The world shifted. My childhood rewrote itself, everything changing as I realized what this room was, what the person-sized, rectangular stone box was. "This is a tomb. This is *my* tomb." I could barely see my parents through my tears, but their smiles hadn't changed.

"Of course," my mother said.

"I'm going to *die*?"

"Everything dies." My mother took a few steps toward me, but I held up my hands, blocking her.

"You don't die! He doesn't die!"

"No, Little Heart, but you—"

"You're going to just let me die? And put me in there, all by myself, forever?"

"You won't be alone. You'll be with your father and all your brothers and sisters who have gone before you."

"But I won't be *here*!"

"No."

"You don't care? That doesn't make you sad? You're not going to do anything to stop it?"

Finally my mother caught on, and her expression softened. "Oh, Isadora, when you understand—"

I ran out of that horrible room. For the first time in my life I *did* understand. All of the stories, the histories I'd been raised on? I had no part in them. My parents brought me into the world to die. They didn't love me enough to keep me forever—they didn't even pretend like they did. My entire childhood of warmth and love was a drawing in the sand—impermanent and fragile and gone in a breath of wind.

Just like me.

Nut, the sky goddess, had disobeyed Amun-Re, god of the sun. She'd taken the god of the earth as a lover. Amun-Re feared that introducing more gods into the world would create an imbalance of power.

Amun-Re put a curse on her that she could not give birth on any day of the year. But Amun-Re did not account for Thoth, gentle god of wisdom and writing. Thoth challenged the Moon herself to a game, and won enough light to create new days. Because those days were not cursed, Nut was able to give birth to Osiris, Isis, Set, and Nephthys.

Osiris, Isis, Set, and Nephthys went on to commit theft, adultery, fratricide, and even attempted murder and extortion against the sun god himself. In retrospect, Amun-Re was probably on to something with that whole "more gods, more chaos" thing.

I FORGET TO ACCOUNT FOR THE TIME OF YEAR when I turn on the sink to scrub the charred remains of the lamb skewers I'm cooking. A torrent of water shoots out, bouncing off the pan and soaking me.

"Chaos!" I shout, furious. I shouldn't even be making dinner. We're having family over, so Mother wants everything to be nice. If she wants it to be nice, *she* should cook. But no. It's summertime. Every summer Isis mourns the death of her beloved husband, and the Nile overflows with her tears. Used to be the whole country would flood, but then they went ahead and dammed the dang thing. That, combined with the lack of worshippers, means now when my mother enters her period of mourning, the only difference you can tell is a substantial increase in water pressure. Awesome for showers, but otherwise pointless.

Still, she uses it as an excuse for everything. Yesterday I asked what was for dinner, and all I heard back were wails for the death of her husband.

Made even more awkward by Father, sitting at the dining room table in his robe and mummy wrappings, reading the paper. Because sure, he was murdered, it sucked, but guess what? Not dead anymore!

I slam the pan back onto the stove and throw new skewers on it. This kitchen was supposed to be ornamental. When I was designing it last year, I never thought I'd actually have to use it. I don't even know how half the state-of-the-art appliances work. They were picked based on color scheme.

Despite a second try, the skewers come out more charred than browned—my mother's efforts to domesticate me foiled yet again.

I throw everything together and balance it on my hip as

I walk out of the kitchen (eggplant walls, shiny black granite counters, sleek black fridge, apparently useless black stove set flat in the counter) and into the dining room. This room is butter yellow with white wood paneling, and a black table to pull in the color theme from the kitchen. The table is perfect: sleek, modern lines, not a scratch on it, one of my best buys ever. It's also occupied by two of my least favorite relatives—Horus, my nightmare know-it-all of an oldest brother, and Hathor, his drunken floozy of a wife.

I slam the platter of charcoal, sauce, and garnishes down in the middle of the table and then sit for dinner. Mother clears her throat primly. She looks strange. Normally she barely gets out of bed during her mourning period, but other than the occasional freakout like yesterday, she's been downright perky.

"Did you pray?" she asks.

"For the last time," I say, narrowing my kohl-lined black eyes at her, "I refuse to pray to my own parents. It's ridiculous."

"Osiris?" My mother looks at him as though he might, for once, step in.

My father slowly turns to the next page of his newspaper. This one's in Tagalog. The whole family is blessed with the gift of tongues (even me), and my father's hobby is reading every newspaper he can find in every language imaginable. No doubt he realizes that newspapers are a dying form. He sympathizes with all things obsolescing and dead. He is the god of the underworld, after all.

I smirk at Mother, knowing that the second she appealed to him I won the argument.

"Very well." She cuts a dainty bite of the blackened mess and chews it, a very nonseasonal smile gradually pulling at her mouth. My mother is beautiful, in a warm, comforting sort of way. Wide hips, full lips, and a bust that inspired art for thousands of years. I'd prefer not to have inherited that from her, but in the grand scheme of things it's not something to complain about. I'm also rocking her same thick, jet-black hair and large almond eyes, though I have heavy bangs that skim my eyelashes and layers that obscure my jawline, strong like Osiris's. Still, no one's making any statues of me.

And no one ever will.

Hathor takes one bite and gags, washing it down with her glass of beer that magically refills itself. She's the *goddess* of beer. And sex. My mother's favorite son married an eternal lush. It'd be funnier if Hathor weren't always slinking around, touching everyone and giving long, lingering looks to anything that moves.

Her dramatic, cat-eye-lined gaze fixes on me. "Essa!" she coos. "This is wonderful."

"It's Isadora."

"Of course!" She laughs, low and intimate. "After all this time I can't keep track anymore! If only your mother would branch out a bit."

Sometimes it hurts to be forgotten while I'm still alive. But she has a point. Every single one of my mother's hundreds of offspring have had variations of her name or my father's. Hathor and Horus (and pretty much everyone else) don't even bother trying to remember my name.

"Nice as always to visit." Hathor smiles at my mother. Or bares her teeth, really.

"It's such a pleasant surprise when I invite my son to a family dinner and you tag along, too." My mother's smile has even more teeth.

After a few tense moments between the two of them, Mother imperiously breaks eye contact. Then she beams at us, clearing her throat over and over again until Osiris finally sets down the paper and looks at her.

"I asked you here for dinner because I have an announcement. I'm pregnant!"

Father blinks slowly, his eyes as black as his skin, then picks the paper back up. "A bit ahead of schedule. What about this one?" He nods in my general direction. I'm too shocked for the *this one* to sting. I'm sixteen. She has a baby every twenty years. Twenty. Not sixteen. Of all of the traditions the goddess of motherhood and fertility could throw out the window, this is the one she picks?

Isis shrugs, trying to look guilty behind her delighted smile. "I thought we could shake things up a bit. Besides, Isadora's getting so big."

"What, I had a growth spurt so now I'm expendable?"

I can't believe she's replacing me already! She could at least pretend I matter even though she didn't care enough to make me last forever like stupid Horus.

I'm so mad about this—I *am*—I'm furious. The only reason there are tears in my eyes is because I used too many onions in dinner. "Besides," I say, trying not to sniffle, "you're the one who's always going on about schedules and traditions and doing things the same way all the time so that chaos can't creep in and mess things up!"

"I think it's wonderful," Horus says, eating with gusto. "Keep the family line going."

I glare at him, knowing exactly what he gets from my mother having more babies. What they all get. I won't pretend otherwise. "Are the batteries running low? Time to pop out a new little worshipper who will be more obedient?"

Mother's glare silences me with a familiar burst of pain. She shakes her head, and the pain eases a bit. "Don't be dramatic, Isadora. You can help me with the baby! It'll be good practice for when you have your own in a few years!"

Oh, death, anything but that. There are enough statues of her nursing miniature pharaohs everywhere I turn that I vowed long ago never to have kids of my own. No squealing babies sucking on my girls *ever*, thankyouverymuch. I quickly wipe under my eyes. Stupid onions.

"You'll be a great help to Mother," Horus says, flashing his falcon-bright eyes at me in a cold smile.

"Gee, thanks, Whore-us." He can't hear how I spell it, but it makes me feel better just knowing.

"When's the new one due to arrive?" he asks our mother, and she beams back, practically glowing now that she is in full maternal-glory mode.

"Two months."

I choke. "Two months? Aren't babies supposed to take, like, four times that long?" I lean back and look at her stomach. Now that I stare, there's a definite bulge. And she's been wearing her flowiest ceremonial robes lately. I hadn't thought anything of it.

"I waited for the right time to tell you. I didn't want to upset you."

"Bang-up job on that one."

"Isadora . . ."

I hold up my hands in surrender. "Fine. Awesome. Two months."

"Another thing," Isis says, her voice getting distant and tight.

I groan. "If you say it's twins, I'm going to stab myself in the eye with this fork."

"I wanted to ask if anyone has had any dreams lately."

The gods all shake their heads, then everyone turns to me.

"Loads of them," I say. "Every night, in fact. It's amazing." Isis's eyes begin narrowing, and I hold up my hands. "Sorry! You'll have to be more specific."

Worry clouds her face. "Dreams of darkness. Dreams of danger."

I shrug. "Nope. Nothing but sunshine and frolicking in the Nile with a herd of purple hippos."

"Purple. Hmm." Her face is way too thoughtful. Never underestimate the ancient Egyptian emphasis on the ability of dreams to portend the future. As far as I'm concerned, a dream is a dream is a dream.

Osiris uses my mother's distraction to stand and drift back to the underworld section of the house, as the others continue talking about the baby news.

I feel a wave of bleak sadness, a desperate, gasping sort of terror. This new life coming to our house forces me to face my own impermanence in a way I try to avoid at all costs. I'm replaceable. Utterly, completely replaceable.

When my first baby tooth falls out as we eat lunch in the ruins of the temple, my mother holds it in the middle of her unlined palm and smiles; her eyes shine with tears, and I worry I've done something wrong.

"It's so small," she says, tucking it carefully into her bag. "When it came in, it looked so big, sitting alone in your tiny pink gums. And it was very, very sharp." She reaches over to deftly twist my long hair in a braid so the wind will quit blowing it into my face.

My tongue darts in and out of the hole that tastes faintly of blood, and I'm fascinated by the new landscape of my mouth, proud that I'm shedding my baby teeth.

"Finish eating quickly, Little Heart. We have to help someone today."

"Why?" I ask, though I know the answer. The repetition is our little game.

"Because it is my job, and you are my special helper. We are defined by what we do for others, so . . ." She taps my nose and raises her eyebrows expectantly.

"So we must have happy, helping hands, and then we'll have happy, helping hearts!"

She beams at me, and the sun shines brighter around us in response, warming me through. "That's my beautiful little girl. If you always let yourself love others, you'll get back more than you give. And that is why I am the happiest mother alive."

"Because you love me." I stand and brush my hands against my bare, knobby knees.

"Because I love you." She kisses my forehead and starts walking toward the dirt road that leads to Abydos's neighborhoods. "There is a woman with a very sick child. We're going to fix both of them. And when we get home, you can help me with some magic before you go see Father."

She's walking quickly and I run to catch up, but my short legs won't cooperate and she's getting farther ahead. And then I remember that my legs aren't short anymore, they're long long long, and I'm not six, and this already happened. But still I can't run, my muscles won't cooperate, and the horizons at the edge of my vision are blurring into black, black that is swirling and eating its way toward my mother, beautiful and oblivious to the danger. She will be swallowed, and I can't let that happen.

The black seems to laugh at me as it curls past, making me complicit in its work, my inaction enabling its destruction. I am an accomplice and it knows it can count on me to simply watch as my mother is destroyed.

I cannot move.

There are as many versions of the myths as there are gods of ancient Egypt.

Amun-Re, king of the gods, had reached his limit with the impudence of humans. Pushed into rage, he called on his Eye to destroy all of humanity. Who was this Eye, capable of ending an entire race? None other than Hathor, who was also Sekhmet, vicious and bloodthirsty goddess of destruction. She killed everything in sight until Amun-Re repented of his wrath. But Hathor-as-Sekhmet could not be stopped. So Amun-Re gathered all the beer in the land and dyed it red, placing it where he knew she'd find it. She was tricked into thinking she'd sated herself on the blood of all the living and fell into a drunken, peaceful stupor.

This is much more like the Hathor I know.

However, this isn't one of the stories I was raised on. My mother taught me the important ones. Meaning the ones she starred in.

I GROAN, THE SOOTHING FINGERS AT MY temple not soothing in the slightest at this hour. "What time is it?"

"Nearly dawn. I need you to help me with some protection amulets. Get up! Quick as a bunny, Little Heart."

Quick as a bunny. I'd like to find the bunny that inspired my mother's favorite saying and skin it alive. I flop over onto my back. My heart settles as I see the constellations mapped out on my ceiling. A few years ago I painted it shimmering black, with twinkle-lit crystals mapping out a chart of the stars on the night I was born. Orion has always been my favorite, right over my bed, watching and protecting me. Sometimes I try to write myself into a constellation, imagine what it would be like to be forever painted across the sky.

I'd be right next to Orion. I smile. I've never called him by the Egyptian name for the constellation. It's one of my few successful rebellions—mostly because my mother doesn't know about it.

"Isadora . . ." Her voice comes out like a song but my muscles start twitching, trying their hardest to obey her against my will. With a final sigh, I throw back my silver comforter and stumble after Isis.

"Did you have any dreams I should know about?" Her face is clouded with worry, distracted as we wind our way to her wing of the house.

A chill rushes over me as I remember my disturbing dream. I had forgotten the memory of losing that tooth. But it's better not to feed her groundless paranoia. "This time the purple hippos had wings."

"Hmmm. Were you frightened of them?"

"Only when they told me an evil woman would wake me up before dawn."

She looks sharply at me. "Really? You saw what would happen?"

I roll my eyes. "No. It's a joke. Sometimes people tell them to each other."

"Dreams are not a joking matter, Isadora."

"Absolutely. Your brain firing off random images while you sleep is dead serious."

"As long as we are agreed."

We enter her workshop, the pale-yellow stone walls always cool, the room flickering from candlelight. Our entire house is underground, about a mile from the remains of a temple in Abydos that tourists still visit. Luckily my parents have enough power to keep away unwanted visitors. Even the entrance is invisible unless you belong here. Most gods barely have the mojo left to stay in physical form, but my parents manage to do some small pieces of magic.

I sigh. "Which one are we doing?"

"Luring and protection."

I heat beeswax over one of the candle flames until it's liquid, then carefully pour it into the vulture mold. Vultures for protection.

"And the hippo," Isis says as she lines up the ivory amulets. "I think your dreams were correct." She places a hand absentmindedly on her stomach.

That's right. Female hippos for Taweret, goddess of childbirth. Floods, I should have picked a different fake dream. I set the molds to the side, grabbing the jar of golden sweet honey. Isis whispers words, the true names of the gods and goddesses that I'm not allowed to know. The wax hardens quickly, and I pop out the miniature animals, setting them up next to each other on the stone table.

I carefully tip the honey onto the figurines, letting it coat them. Sweetness to lure out evil spirits, then trap them in the protective animals.

Yup. Sure. Beeswax and honey to combat bad dreams. Just some more early-morning mother-daughter bonding time in the House of Life.

Isis finishes whispering names to the ivory pendants, then drapes one around my neck. I clench my jaw, feeling the rough leather cord on my skin, the ivory warmer than it should be. "Do I need one?"

"Of course, my heart." She drapes another over her own neck, clutching a third in her hand. The wax figures are left where they are. "This should be sufficient. Thank you, Isadora. Don't be afraid. The baby will be a good thing. It will give us something to do together." Her voice is odd. Almost . . . vulnerable. And she's avoiding my eyes.

A soft noise, so quiet I nearly miss it, sounds behind us and I turn to find my aunt Nephthys, half hidden by the doorframe.

"Come in," my mother says, barely looking at her sister. "Isadora can help with anything you need. Horus asked me to make breakfast." She smiles as she swishes out of the room.

Nephthys hovers over my mother's workroom table, flitting from stone jars to ceramic containers of herbs, spices, and dungs, her hands dancing nervously like two wounded birds. She nods to herself sometimes, but doesn't ask me what anything is for. She's helped my mother a lot, kind of an assistant through the ages. Lucky me, I inherited that role as soon as I was old enough.

I lean against the wall, wishing I were back in bed.

Then she surprises me. "How are you?" she asks. I hardly even know what her voice sounds like. She's always been on the edges, there my whole life, but never really connecting. Just *there*.

"Umm, tired?"

"You seem unhappy." Her voice is barely above a whisper, as tentative as her trembling hands when she twists a fingertip through the thick, golden honey. "Do you help your mother in here often?"

"Yeah, all the time."

"Can you decipher her handwriting?" She lifts the corner of one of my mother's papyruses, the cramped and flowing glyphs there a language in and of themselves. Since it's a written language of my mother's own making, though, the gift of tongues does not apply.

I give a halfhearted shrug. "Yeah. Took me a long time to learn, but I can read anything she writes. Very useful life skill, there."

"Hmmm." She licks the honey off her finger. If Hathor

19

did it, it'd be like something from a music video, all tongue and sexy eyes. But Nephthys darts her tongue out like the honey will burn her, sucks her finger like it's bleeding. "I don't think your mother understands you." She offers me a thin smile, her eyes watery.

I'm shocked. No one notices me enough to get that I'm not happy, and my mom is oblivious. "No," I say, "she doesn't."

Nephthys nods, looking into a corner along the ceiling. "Time and distance, I think, might be good."

Her words stun me. Is she on my side? Could she talk my mom into sending me away before my eighteenth birthday? I need to get out, now more than ever.

"I couldn't agree more." I bite my lip, then go for it. "It'd help if someone else convinced my mom of the same thing."

"Oh. Oh. Well. I don't . . . Isis is so . . . Perhaps I could say something? Soon. Maybe when the baby comes. Or after. It's not my place, and . . . I will try to say something. Soon."

I slouch, deflated. I can't pin any hopes on this timid shell of a god. Compared to my mother, Nephthys is a shadow.

Leaving her alone, I walk out into the still-dark hall. Maybe with precious Whore-us here I can get a few more hours of sleep in before my mother realizes I am being lazy and gives me something productive to do.

Or maybe I'll use this free time to plot how to escape. I'm lost in thoughts of sneaking out while my mom gives birth when something muffled and strange, a noise that doesn't belong, comes from the other direction and I whip around.

There are two people tangled together. The sound is . . . oh, idiot gods, it's their mouths slurping at each other. Thank you, Hathor and Whore-us. I'm about to run and bleach my eyeballs when I realize—those pointy features? The face that still carries a hint of predator? That is not the falcon-proud face of my brother.

That is the jackal-mean face of Anubis. Who has been banned from the main house since I was a kid. And who is now sucking face with Whore-us's wife.

I try to sneak down the hall unnoticed but freeze when a voice I thought I'd forgotten hits a spot between my shoulder blades, making me tense up. A memory tickles, something about why he was banished from our house, but I cannot for the life of me remember. "Good morning, little one." I turn to find Anubis right behind me, looming and leering. "Not so little anymore, though."

I back up a step. Anubis is handsome, his features all sharp cunning, with a hint of cruelty to his eyes and the twist of his mouth. His ears are high and almost pointed.

"Oh, uh, hey. What are you doing here?"

"Visiting my domain, as is my right."

My nose stings this close to him. Being the god of embalming doesn't make you smell very nice. "Yeah, cool. Well, you know where to find my father."

"*Our* father." His teeth snap on the words, and he leans in, his eyes focused in the region lower than my face. "You are definitely not so little anymore."

Floods, is Anubis *hitting* on me?

For once the sound of my mother's shriek is music to my ears. "What are you doing here? You are not welcome."

Nephthys comes into the hall from the workroom. Her eyes go wide when she sees her son, and she squeaks with panic.

"Did you bring him?" my mother demands, and I have a headache from the aftershock of her voice.

"No! No, I—no!" Nephthys backs away, not looking at any of us.

Hathor giggles from the dim back corner of the long hall, then sways her hips as she walks toward us. "Relax. He's family, right?" From my vantage point I see Hathor trace a finger along Anubis's arm.

But his hungry black eyes are still on me.

My mother must notice, too, because without looking at me she says, "Isadora. Go to your room. Now."

That had been my plan, but now I want to see what's going on here. And I really want to see Hathor get it for hanging out with Anubis. "But I—"

"NOW!" Her voice shoves me down the hall, and I trip and run into my room, slamming the door behind me.

My mother follows after a few short minutes, looking harried and distracted. "I need to know exactly what you have been dreaming of."

"I can't remember." I look anywhere but at her. She'll know I'm lying. She always knows. When I was little, it got to the point that if I even thought about doing something naughty, I'd get a headache anticipating her disapproving glare. She lets out a small noise like a hum, then puts her hand on her stomach.

"I do not like Anubis's reappearance in our home, or the way he was looking at you. Normally I wouldn't worry, but a woman is never more vulnerable than when she is with child and giving birth." She sounds genuinely concerned.

I roll my eyes. "Yeah, but you're not a woman. You're a goddess." I barely manage to avoid tacking on a *so shut up about it already*.

"Have you learned that little from our family history?"

"You mean lessons on incest? Betrayal? Jealousy? Murder? It doesn't count as dying if you come back to life, which everyone always managed to do."

"It is not myself I am worried about." She reaches out and takes my hand with a strange, frightened intensity, and suddenly, in spite of my insistence that dreams are only dreams, I really, really want to know what hers have been about. Or I really, really don't. I can't decide.

"Well, I think I'm pretty safe. Who would care enough to hurt me?" In the grand scheme of things, I don't matter. At all.

"With the baby coming, I worry. I can't watch you. I should have known Anubis was in our temple, but I didn't even feel him." She reaches up and takes a strand of my long black hair between her fingers. "I wanted this baby to be something we did together, to bridge the gulf between us. To make us a family again."

I grit my teeth. She's such a liar. She only has babies to serve her own selfish purposes.

She lets go of my hair, nods like she's come to a decision. "I won't have you in danger. Which is why I'm sending you away."

"Wait, you're—what? You're sending me away? That's not fair! That's—" That's exactly what I want. Hope rises, lumping in my throat and threatening to choke me. "Okay," I manage to squeak out.

"Nephthys mentioned it just now when I confided my worries. She thinks it would be for the best."

I want to pump my fist in the air, to jump up and down on my bed. Nephthys, silent slouching Nephthys, actually came through for me!

"You should be safe at Horus's."

"*No. No way.* I will not go live with Whore-us!"

"I need to know you're safe and that I don't have to worry about you."

"Well, I'm certainly not going to be safe with Whore-us! He can't even remember my name; what makes you think he's going to watch out for me? And besides, you want me to spend all my time with Hathor?"

"I don't know," she says, her voice drifting off, worry clipping its edges.

I am winning. Idiot gods, *I am going to win.* This is the first time in my entire life I have been able to push my mother on an issue and actually get her to budge. I take a deep breath, determined not to blow it.

"If you're going to send me away to keep me safe, you should *really* send me away. Somewhere far away, away from the gods, away from Egypt. If no one knows where I am except for you, I couldn't be any safer, could I?"

"It's out of the question. You are too young to go anywhere on your own."

No, I can still make this happen. I have to. "You're absolutely right." I try to sound nervous, hesitant about leaving her. "If only we knew someone who lived outside of Egypt and was out of contact with everyone here."

I gag on the thickness of my own hint. Please come to the same conclusion, Mother. Please.

"Hmm. There is Sirus."

"Sirus?" I should win some sort of an award for the delicate inflection of surprise I weave through my voice.

"You remember Sirus, don't you? He hasn't been to visit since you were small."

Of course I remember Sirus. He's my favorite brother, the closest in age to me and the only nonweirdo. Sirus did it right. When he turned eighteen and was set free, he cut ties completely, moving to San Diego.

"Yeah, I remember him. I guess that'd work, right? All the other gods have forgotten he even exists. And he's really responsible."

She frowns. "He drives cars for a living." My mother thinks cars are distasteful. All that metal and plastic without personality or intelligence. Not much money in the chariot business, though.

I don't answer. I hold my breath, keeping it caught in my chest with my hopes.

Finally she sighs. "I think it might be for the best. Only for the next two months, until the baby comes."

I exhale so loudly she jumps, startled. On the inside I am screaming, spinning in dizzy circles, bidding my Egyptian prison farewell forever, because one thing is certain: Once I make it out of here, I am never, *ever* coming back. I will no longer be a temporary guest checked into the Hotel of the Gods.

My voice is utterly calm when I finally speak. "Okay. If you think it's best."

"I hope it's best. But you should go ask your father first, just in case."

And the part of my brain that is still jumping on the bed screaming in triumph trips and face-plants into the floor. Because now the only thing standing between me and the freedom I've been dreaming of for the last three years is a quick trip to the underworld.

I nearly bump into old Thoth in the hallway. He's here

26

often, in a quiet, slightly senile old geezer capacity, and he's always been my favorite. "You look sad," Thoth says, his wobbly voice soft. His neck is cricked in the middle, bringing to mind the ibis he was often drawn as. He winks one small, deep-set eye at me, bringing a hand up and turning it into a bird head, which also winks at me. He used to do puppet shows with his hands, having the "bird-ies" tell me the stories of my heritage, like the time the Earth knocked up the Sky and my parents were born. I loved it. When I was eight. I roll my eyes but try to force a halfhearted smile for his effort.

"Gotta go see Osiris," I say, and Thoth steps aside with a quiet shuffle. I hesitate at the top of the worn stone steps. I haven't been here for so long. There's a special scent to this place—not terrible, not even unpleasant, but distinct. No rotting, just age. Weight. The passage of centuries and millennia marches unmeasured beneath the earth. The Sun comes and goes in his eternal cycle, but the dust and air and stones here take no notice.

I reach up a hand to trail along the rough stone at the bottom of the stairs. It shocks me how . . . small it feels. Now I'm less than half a meter beneath the ceiling.

Two more turns and straight past the room where I spent so much of my childhood. I don't look in, but my chest tightens as I leave it behind. Finally the end of the passage. The great room, high ceilinged, with murals in blacks and reds and blues telling the stories of Egypt. I thought they were my stories, but I'm not even a footnote.

My dad sits ramrod straight on his low-backed, elaborately carved throne. He holds two staffs, his white atef crown towering over his head, and observes his kingdom with eyes that can't see me right now. I shiver, wondering if anyone's actually here on their journey into the afterlife. I stick to the side of the room just in case. And to avoid Ammit, sitting in the middle of the room looking for all the world like a bizarre statue—head of a crocodile, front legs of a lion, and rear half of a hippo. She is silent and still, jaws awaiting the hearts of the unjust dead.

I stand in front of Osiris, who doesn't respond. I clear my throat.

"Father? Father!"

Nothing changes. Anger flares up in my chest, and I'm tempted to grab one of his silly staffs and knock off his stupid crown with it. But I don't want to touch him, not when he's like this, so far removed from me. So . . . dead.

"OSIRIS."

Finally he blinks, eyes slowly focusing on me. "Child. You've come back?"

Ah, floods, he thinks I'm here to work on my tomb. I straighten my shoulders. "I'm leaving. Going to live with Sirus because Isis thinks it's not safe here for me until after she has the baby." I pause, but he doesn't react. He could still blow this whole thing for me. "Er, if it's okay with you."

I think for a minute that there's a trace of sadness in his eyes, but then again, he always looks serious and mournful.

He nods slowly. "If that is the path your mother feels is best. But you will return home when the time comes?"

It's physically painful to hold back my eye roll, but I can control my attitude long enough to get out of here. "Yup, sure, I'll be back."

He nods, satisfied. "Go well, little one."

That's it? I just told him I'm leaving to live somewhere else, and all I get is a *go well*? I thought I'd be elated, but instead I'm disappointed. "Are you going to miss me at all?"

He smiles, his stiff features resisting the movement. "We will have eternity. I can let you go for these few heartbeats."

No. Once I step out that door, I'm gone forever.

A small, aching part of me is sure my parents won't care either way. They won't notice that I never come back. They'll probably forget my name. Maybe my father already has.

I turn around and leave, glancing back and hating myself for it. His eyes have gone blank, seeing only his real home, the real world he loves. Chaos take him. I'm done.

I play in the sand on the banks of the Nile, scratching out the glyphs I'm just barely learning while my mother searches for the best reeds and dirt for our spells that day. A shadow blocks the sun and I look up to see tall, tall Anubis.

"Hello, whelp of Isis," he says, and I admire his teeth and wish mine were sharper. My new front ones are starting to grow in, but they're just big and bumpy.

"Hi."

"Do you know how to swim?" he asks.

"No."

"Time to learn!" He picks me up, lifting me high, so high in the air, and then throws me straight out into the middle of the river before I can even process what is happening.

I sink. I've never been in the water without my mother before, and she isn't here, and I don't know what to do without her. I look wildly around, the water murky and stinging my eyes, but I know if I wait, my mother will come for me.

She has to. She always comes for me.

When my chest hurts so much I want to cry and I can't hold

my breath any longer, the water turns inky, creeping black.

No hands pull me out. Hands were supposed to come—they came, I remember they came, but . . .

Everything turns black, and I can't breathe, I can't breathe, I can't—

Amun-Re ruled over the other gods, preeminent and most powerful. But someone needed to fill the throne of god-king of Egypt, where war and cannibalism reigned supreme. The country needed peace.

Osiris was made god-king of Egypt, with Isis (who still talks about how fabulous her outfits were during this era) by his side. Together they taught the people proper worship and ushered in an era of unprecedented order.

Probably they should have worried more about how his brother, Set, god of chaos, would feel about this turn of events.

I SHIVER IN THE EXCESSIVE AIR-CONDITIONING of the San Diego airport. Everything is shiny and sleek and cool, all white and chrome and lifeless. Neon signs for food that makes my stomach turn with its smell flash at me as I hurry down the huge hall, looking for the exit. For a few seconds I long to be on one of my rare trips outside to the open-air market near my home, in the dust and heat and shouting chaos. The energy there is palpable, the city a living thing. The colors, the noises—it feels like a heartbeat, like art. Here, it feels like money.

I hope this isn't what all of America is like.

But I don't want to go back to Egypt, not ever. I'm just tired beyond belief. I didn't sleep at all on the flights, and I'm loopy with exhaustion.

I'm glad to be here. Thrilled. America has no culture. There's no weight of history, barely even centuries to pull on people. You can be whoever and whatever you want, genealogy and history and religion as fleeting and unimportant as the latest trend in style that'll be gone as quickly as it came.

America has no roots. Nothing here lasts forever. I'll fit right in.

My goose-pimpled arms make me wish that instead of luggage I'd been able to bring my mother's bag. She always has exactly what anyone might need: a snack or a cardigan or a tampon or antivenin, so on and so forth.

I turn the corner and the airport opens up, the escalators leading to the bottom level with baggage claim and huge windows dark with night. I go down, looking around, and there he is.

Sirus's hair is perfect, shiny black, cut close to his head. He has my same strong, straight nose, but he wears glasses over his dark eyes. No way you'd guess he was actually thirty-six. He looks midtwenties, tops. My heart leaps, happy and excited to see him, to have something familiar in this strange new place. He sees me and grins, waving with his free arm.

Which is when I notice his other arm around a beautiful

black woman with a head of wild corkscrew curls, a sleeve-less dress, and a huge, huge, huge pregnant belly.

Floods, babies are *taking over the world.*

A sharp sting of betrayal flares in my stomach, and I can't hold back my scowl. What is Sirus thinking? So much for his free and independent life. And he didn't even tell me! Not a single mention of a girlfriend, much less a baby on the way.

I manage to wipe my scowl away and force a smile by the time I get to the bottom, though I'm sick inside. Nothing here feels like what I thought it would.

"Baby sister!" Sirus picks me up and twirls me around in a hug even though I'm nearly his height. I laugh in spite of my anger, shocked more than anything by human contact. I honestly can't remember the last time someone hugged me. I haven't let my mother hug me in years. It feels strange. It feels nice.

"Isadora, this is Deena, my wife." He grins, bursting with pride as he sets me down and looks at her. She smiles—it lights up her whole face—and, much to my shock, wraps her arms around me in an awkward, belly-filled hug. Her head barely hits my shoulders. This hug is not so nice. I don't know where to put my arms, or what to do, or why this woman I didn't even know existed is suddenly hugging me.

"I'm so happy to meet you, Isadora! Sirus has told me so much about you. I've always been sad that I couldn't meet his family, and I'm thrilled that it worked out for you to come stay with us!"

I smile fakely, glancing at Sirus for support. How much did he tell her?

He winks. "Deena knows all about how our family is deeply religious and won't leave Egypt, so it's better for you to come here before you apply to American universities in a couple of years."

I let out a breath. "Yeah. That whole religion thing. Gods are so overrated."

Deena laughs, weaving her arm through mine. "Well, I'm thrilled. I've never had a sister, but always wanted one. Plus, Sirus tells me you're an interior decorator."

"Designer," I correct before realizing it makes me sound rude. "I mean, I kind of think of it more as art." My projects around the house were my salvation these last couple of years. I think that's what I'd like to do with my life. Take blank spaces and make them beautiful. Create something where nothing was before, where I can control every aspect of it.

"Exactly! That's so great. And I'm apologizing, because I'm going to put you to work right away to earn your keep. Our house is in desperate need of room art." She smiles warmly, and I think I might like her. As soon as I find out what the crap Sirus was thinking, getting married and not telling me about it.

We work our way through the crowds to the luggage

35

pickup. Deena's amazed by my flawless, accent-free English. She should hear my Afrikaans; it's awesome. I find out she is a city attorney and they've been married for *two years*. I kick Sirus covertly in the shins when he says that, as punishment for being a big fat liar and hiding things from me. What is *wrong* with him?

"It's so sad that your parents wouldn't come to the wedding because they can't leave Egypt." Deena shakes her head sympathetically and I nod, assuming Sirus will let me in on whatever elaborate mythology he's created to explain our family. He should have just said they were dead, since in our father's case it's technically true.

The belts start turning, and looking out for my luggage saves me from any more conversation. The first few suitcases come down the ramp, and my stomach sinks. They are all black. And midsized. And look exactly like mine. I flash back to my last afternoon with my mother, picking out luggage. She told me not to get black because it would look like everyone else's. I ignored her because she's never traveled by plane. How did she know? How does she always know?

After pulling no fewer than four wrong suitcases, I finally find mine. Sirus grabs it and we head outside. It's dark, and my stomach is unsettled from all of the change and startling revelations. The air is cool, wetter than I'm used to. I can feel it on my skin, pawing at me, and I don't like it. I look expectantly at the sky, needing to see my stars.

"It's cloudy," I say, my voice small and sad.

"June gloom," Deena answers. "San Diego has amazing weather year-round, but June has almost constant cloud cover. Still, it means the beaches aren't as crowded."

I nod, not caring about the beach, and we find Sirus's tiny Mini. It's sky blue, old but perfectly maintained. I love it. I'd paint it cherry red with racing stripes. It makes me happy that even though he runs a fleet of limos and taxis, my brother drives this.

"Sorry about the space," he says, opening the back to shove my suitcase in.

"Poor Sirus," Deena says, a smile pulling at her lips. "He's finally going to have to give up driving his baby because he's having a baby."

"I still say we could fit."

"I'm not dealing with a car seat in a two-door."

Sirus sighs heavily, opening the passenger door and flipping the seat forward so I can climb into the back. "Want a car, Isadora?"

I laugh, nervous, as I buckle my seat belt and try to fold my long legs in such a way that they won't be slammed up against the driver's seat. "Umm, I've barely even ridden in cars. I don't exactly know how to drive them."

"We can work on that. In the meantime, Deena has a bike she's not using."

"Thanks." I don't know how to ride a bike, either, but

that has less potential for killing innocent bystanders.

He starts the car but pauses to take Deena's hand and pull it to his lips in a surprisingly intimate and affectionate gesture.

I look outside, uncomfortable. This isn't how it was supposed to be. I don't feel free; I feel nervous and edgy and out of place. Sirus wasn't supposed to have his own family. *I* was supposed to be his family. Instead I'm just going to be another footnote to someone else's story.

I'll be fine. I'm always fine. But I'm disappointed. Not even Orion is around to care about me here.

The blank whiteness above sends me into a momentary panic. I'm in another nightmare. No. Sirus's house. I was so tired when we got here last night, it was all I could do to take my boots off before collapsing into bed.

Floods, the ceiling is *so white*. I push back the heavy comforter and am greeted by a seeping chill in the air. Apparently Southern California is not as warm as I thought it would be. I brush my arms, feeling like they should be wet, but they're just cold. Shivering, I wrap up in a soft blue throw draped on the edge of the bed. My bare legs stretch out about a foot past the bottom of the blanket, but it'll do for now.

Sirus and Deena live in an area called Ocean Beach— or Pacific Beach—or Something or Other Beach, which I suspect could be the name of every community here. It's a mess of homes built into the hills, and theirs is a great gray rambling wood confusion of a house.

The whole thing is pleasant but a complete *nothing* designwise, all white and beige, and already my mind is spinning with the potential. I think this will be the beach room. The dark wood floors I'm not touching—they're perfect—but I want a seaweed-green throw rug, the walls palest yellow, and a light sea-green ceiling.

The accents will all be glass. I'll troll the local shops for glass artisans; surely they have that type of shop here. Blown-glass vases, or ideally some sort of abstract art that looks like kelp. Maybe a painting or two in ocean blues and greens. The bedspread I'll keep white, but with a shock of bright coral-orange pillows.

I'm totally going to earn my keep. My feet pad along the cold wood floors with an extra spring. None of last night's melancholy will be allowed—today is mine. Tomorrow is mine. Every day from now until I die? Mine.

"What do you mean I have a *job*?" I stare at Sirus in horror.

He clutches the newspaper in front of him like a shield. When I walked in and saw him sitting at his (awful, awful maple with Queen Anne chairs) table reading the paper, the resemblance to our father was uncanny. Except Sirus has no mummy wrappings. However, the momentary surge of affection I felt for him has entirely disappeared.

"I thought she told you." He takes off his glasses and rubs the space between his eyes. "When she asked if you could stay with me, she had some rules."

"SHE IS NOT HERE. SHE CANNOT CONTROL MY LIFE."

"Isadora. Sit down and hear me out, okay?"

I slump into a chair across from him, deflating. I shouldn't yell at him. It's not his fault our mother can't understand that not even *her* divine apron strings can stretch all the way from Egypt to San Diego.

"Okay, hit me. What does the Queen of Heaven think I should be doing?"

"Pancakes!" Deena says, sashaying into the dining room. Her hair is even wilder this morning, curls everywhere, and everything about her seems to imitate them—she is all movement and light and energy. If it weren't for that *thing* in her belly and the fact that she stole my brother from me, I'd think she was awesome.

I kick Sirus under the table for good measure.

"Hope this is okay." Deena sets a plate down on the table and then sits with an ungraceful *oof*. "And don't get used to it. Weekdays I am gone by seven and you are on your own."

I've never had pancakes before. I wait, watching what Deena does to prepare hers, my stomach growling. This is not the wholesome, basic fare my mother insists on. I spear a golden pancake and plop it onto my plate, then drench it in syrup. I can smell it—pure sugar and artificial flavoring. My mother says if you can't pronounce all of the ingredients, it shouldn't go in your body.

I say, *Sugar, yay!*

The paint here is white, again, some more. Cutouts in the wall open to the kitchen. I like those. But I want to curve the top of them so they're arches, not rectangles. I don't think severe and modern is the right fit for Deena and Sirus. They need a warm home, a soft home, a home that is beautiful and safe and a bit funky.

The kitchen has nice appliances, dark granite counters. I want neutral pale-green tiles as backsplashes on the walls between the counters and cupboards, which need to be painted either cherry or white. White, I think, once we get rid of all the rest of the white. We'll shop for handles and put different ones on each cupboard. Pewter, or dark silver.

"Do you work a lot?" I ask Deena around a sticky-sweet mouthful. I can feel it coating my throat, clinging there, and it's actually a bit overwhelming but I soldier on, determined to enjoy eating something Mother wouldn't approve of.

Deena nods. "Not as much as I would if I were at a firm, but I keep busy."

I have no idea what a city attorney does, but it sounds cool. And very . . . worky. No wonder he kept her secret. My mother is all about industry but utterly and completely opposed to married women in the workforce. She'd never approve of Sirus's choice if she knew that Deena was employed at anything other than perfect domesticity.

"Awesome. Speaking of jobs?" I jab my fork toward Sirus. Might as well find out.

"Oh, right. Mom loaned a bunch of stuff to a new exhibit at a local museum. She set you up with a job there to oversee everything."

I snort, choking on a piece of pancake. "Oh, that's perfect. I finally get away, so she plots to have me spend all day every day staring at pictures of her and Father?"

Sirus widens his eyes at me, and I look at Deena who, fortunately, is tapping out a message on her phone. Whew. "I mean, staring at pictures they donated? Ha. Like that's going to happen. I wanted to talk to you about which room I can start on. Maybe this area? I love how open everything is. How do you feel about a slowly shifting palette that will incorporate movement—almost like a tide that carries the eye from the entry to the family room to the dining room? Also, how attached are you to this table? Because I'm thinking bonfire."

Sirus shakes his head, black eyes crinkling up with a smile. "Umm, no fires. But I'm serious about the job thing."

"And I'm serious that Mother's crazy. She's not here, I'm not doing it."

"She said you'd say that. And she told me to say—and please remember that I am only passing this along because you are a minor and I don't have legal custody—that if you don't do the job, she's taking everything out of your bank account."

I play with the remaining syrup on my plate, stirring it around with my fork. "So what? I'll get a real job. I'm not afraid to work." I don't care what it is. Anything's better than what *she* wants me to do.

Deena looks up from her phone with an apologetic frown. "You can't get a job, not legally anyway. You don't have the right type of visa. And while there are a lot of jobs for illegals here, I really doubt you want to stand on a corner at Home Depot and get picked up for daily construction work."

I frown, torn. I *am* pretty strong. Maybe I could. . . .

"Don't tell her that's an option," Sirus whispers, doing the kill motion across his throat.

"If you violate your visa," Deena continues hurriedly, "you risk getting kicked out of the country permanently. Plus Sirus and I would be breaking the law if we helped you work illegally, which frankly wouldn't look good on my record."

I throw my hands in the air. "Then how is it okay for me to work at the museum?"

Sirus shrugs. "Because they aren't technically employing you. You're a volunteer. With regularly scheduled hours. And mandatory attendance that will be reported directly to Mom."

"And that's the only way I have access to any money at all."

"Sorry, kiddo. We'd support you, but—"

"No, I don't want that." I scowl and trace the grain of the wood on the table. "I don't want to be any sort of burden on you. I'll do the stupid job." I stand, and I can see the mixture of relief and regret on Sirus's face. "But seriously? I *am* going to burn this table. Now if you'll excuse me, I need to get some air." It's hard to breathe with my mother's tentacles reaching out to strangle me from across the world, after all.

I stare at the mural of my parents' creation, Grandma Nut arching across the sky. I reach up, standing on my tiptoes, to trace my finger along her length. I don't understand why I can't visit her, can't see her like I can so many aunts and uncles.

I turn to go back to my room when I run into a pair of legs and look up to see Set. I freeze, terrified as always.

"Hello, child," he says, and his voice is soft and calm as he bends down to be eye level with me. He looks so much like my father, except Set's skin is healthy brown, not corpse black like Osiris's.

I swallow and stammer hello, which embarrasses me because I'm nearly nine and I don't stutter now.

"Why are you sad?" he asks.

I'm not sad, not anymore. Now I'm scared. But I answer, "Because Grandma Nut isn't here and I can't see her. I don't understand why." I scowl, try to stand taller in defiance. It's not fair. "Why are you still here, but she isn't?"

Set's smile is in his eyes. "Do you understand that only the gods who are remembered or worshipped—even inadvertently— are strong enough to remain in physical form?"

I nod, but I don't know what *inadvertently* means.

"You should study current events," he says, standing tall again. "Then you will know why the god of chaos still walks the earth and never needs fear oblivion." He smiles again, and it frightens me.

I turn to run down the hall to where my mother is, but it's blank, an empty black space, and I know she won't be there. I back slowly away, past Set, past the mural, where my mother's image has been erased.

Everything is wrong. This is all wrong.

||
||

Set was not well pleased with his brother's ascension to god-king of Egypt.

"A game," Set declared, bringing out a beautiful chest. "We will see who fits the best."

Osiris was a perfect fit. Unsurprising, because it was a coffin specially made for him. Set seized it, sealed it, and condemned Osiris to a slow death. He dumped the coffin into the Nile, surrendering it to the depths and denying Osiris a proper burial and entry into the afterlife.

Isis would not allow this. She searched the river and the sea until she found the coffin and brought it back to Egypt to prepare for burial. But clever, vengeful Set found where she had hidden it and chopped his brother's body into fourteen pieces.

Ever faithful, Isis and her sister Nephthys searched all of Egypt and found . . . thirteen pieces. The fourteenth, Osiris's penis, had been eaten by a fish. Industrious and undeterred, Isis just made him a new one. That magical penis went on to sire Horus, who carried on the good fight against Set and chaos. It also made Anubis.

It also made me, but let's not think about that.

SIRUS DRIVES UP THE MIDDLE OF THE CITY, which is built on a series of hills looking out over the harbor. Most of the skyscrapers are farther south, but I love the mixture of tall buildings and turn-of-the-century homes preserved in the middle. Everything is bright, and there's so much metal and so many signs. I wonder how anyone finds anything here. Yesterday I went into a grocery store and was so overwhelmed I turned around and walked right back out. They have everything there in the same place. Once you started, how would you ever leave?

I thought watching the occasional American film and television series would prepare me to live here. I was wrong. And it sucks. But I refuse to be homesick. I will make wherever I am my home. Or I'll have no home at all. Either is better than living in a past and future where I don't belong.

"How did you keep Deena a secret from Mother?" I ask as we wait at a light.

"Hmm? Oh, Mom knows about her. She wasn't thrilled about me starting my family here instead of Egypt, but we've had that fight so many times over the years, I think I've finally worn her down."

I frown. This doesn't make any sense. I was under the impression that Sirus didn't have any contact with Isis at all. Maybe his lack of video chatting has more to do with his painful tech unsavviness than actually avoiding talking to her. "Why didn't you tell *me*?"

He shrugs, looking uncomfortable. "I thought it was more important that you talk to me about the things you needed to when you called. I just kind of never got around to it."

That's a crap excuse if I've ever heard one. What he's saying is he's been pretending to understand me all these years, while secretly talking to our mother even though he doesn't have to, and sneaking around behind my back, getting married and starting a family. Parenthood is self-ish. There's no reason to bring a child into the world other than that *you* want one for your own self-centered reasons. His can't be as bad as our parents', but still.

"And Mother's okay with Deena? Even with the whole working thing?"

"Yeah, of course. I mean, she's a little concerned that Deena isn't going to quit after the baby comes, but she trusts us to figure it out."

"Are we talking about the same woman?"

Sirus laughs. "You know, she's not nearly as crazy and controlling as you act like she is."

"You say, driving me to a job I didn't ask for and don't want but am being forced to do." I scowl out the window. Whose side is he on?

We cross an intersection into a grassy park area and then over a bridge to another world. It's as though they've built a city within the city—the buildings aren't tall, but they're all beautiful, things from another time and place. Elaborate sculptures are carved right into the walls, and we drive through onto a cobbled street, the buildings themselves arching over the entrance.

"That's your museum," Sirus says, pointing to the first building. I have time to see huge, blue doors, intricately carved and surrounded by concrete stairs, before we're through another underpass and into a roundabout. "I have a bit of an emergency this morning—not enough drivers—so is it okay if I drop you off here?" He pulls over into a handicapped parking area.

Suddenly I'm nervous, which I hate. I have nothing to be nervous about. I didn't ask for this, and I don't care what they think of me. I have half a mind to "accidentally" knock over a bust of my mother.

And then dance on the shards.

Still, my stomach flutters. "They're expecting me, right?"

Sirus grins. "Like Mom would forget to follow up. I'll be back at four. Chin up, kiddo. It'll be fun."

"Party," I mutter, and climb out. The road weaves away past an outdoor amphitheater in the same pale stonework as most of the buildings. Everything is surrounded by green, bright explosions of flowers, and the odd fountain. There doesn't appear to be much sense to the buildings, but a broad, pedestrian-only street leads the opposite direction of my museum. I'll have to explore later. I like how this place is sheltered from the crush of cars and the endless rows of houses and buildings.

Though there *are* still crowds wandering around. I feel

claustrophobic. Who knew that living in the real world included so many *people*?

I walk down the covered sidewalk, past some bizarre modern sculptures in a garden, craning my neck when the roof opens up to see the domed tower atop the museum, accented with blue and yellow tile. A bell chimes the time. Almost late.

I walk slower.

But not slow enough, and even dragging my feet up the stairs brings me to the doors just as they open. A tiny, energetic brunette flashes me a brilliant smile. Her eyes are about even with my chest. My relative height here keeps surprising me, too. Even after my painful growth spurt, I was always the shortest, other than stooped Thoth.

Here I am tall. Really tall. Of course, my spike heels propelling me well past my 1.8 meters probably help. I enjoy it, though. I feel like I can breathe better.

"You must be Isadora!"

I hold my hands out in a silent ta-da motion.

"I'm Michelle! We're so excited that you'll be with us this summer. Museum traffic swings up so much—especially once schools go on break in the next couple of weeks. It's always nice to have extra hands, and with your background, well! It's going to be great. And I can't even begin to tell you how thrilled we are about your parents' incredible donation of their traveling exhibit." She's practically bouncing up and down. I see why my mother picked her—she's even wearing an ankh necklace under her nice white button-down blouse.

I'm dressed in a black pencil skirt and a cherry-red top, my hair down, stick straight, my thick bangs so long they almost cover my eyes. I debated this morning whether or not to show up in jeans and a tee, torn between rebelliously refusing to adhere to the dress code and being nice. But it isn't the museum's fault my mother's a control freak.

I'm entertained by the way Michelle chops her hands through the air as she's explaining the plan for a separate wing when the exhibit arrives, and how she prefaces many of her sentences with, "I mean, *look*." Unfortunately, if I cave and like anything about this (including Michelle), my mother wins.

Conundrums.

We walk past a circular lobby with double desks and into a massive main room, the ceiling open to the top of the building. The second-floor balcony wraps all the way around and lets in natural light from huge, round-top windows, and the middle of the floor down here showcases massive carved stone pillars. Michelle cheerily tells me about this exhibit on ancient Mesoamericans, its history, how long it'll stay up. I've never heard anyone talk so fast in my entire life. She packs more words into a single breath than most people do in five.

We head up the stairs, past some exhibit on the origins of humankind, and over to the Egyptian room. The entrance is deep purple and green, with gold lettering. The colors are all wrong, really. I appreciate the effort to make it look regal, but I'd have done it differently.

The actual exhibit is shockingly small—a single room, with cases on the sides and in the middle. I'm greeted by a cartoon version of my creepy, lecherous half brother Anubis, which makes me giggle.

Michelle turns to me midsentence. "What?"

I shake my head. "Oh, nothing. Sorry. Go on." Cartoon Anubis is pointing to the centerpiece of the room—a headless mummy. We have better in our tombs at home. But it's a decent collection for such a small museum. And there's a whole case of things from Abydos, one of which is allegedly from the tomb of Osiris. It's kind of adorable they think someone could find the tomb of a god.

"The Children's Discovery Room is through those doors," Michelle says, pointing to a set of double doors with a sign across declaring the exhibit closed. "It'll open up later, and is one of our most popular rooms. There's a video presentation on the mummification process narrated by Anubis. You'll love it!"

"I'm sure I will." I can see it now: Anubis leering and smirking, sharp eyes and sharp teeth with a smile curled around them. Because he's totally the most kid friendly of the gods. I know the jackal-headed jerk is the god of embalming, but really, for children? They should have Thoth with his birdie hands.

"If you'll familiarize yourself with the room, I'm going to give you some extra reading to do so you can answer any questions that people might have, but I'm guessing that, with your parents, you're already something of an expert." She pauses, looking at me with a cocked head. "You know, put on a headdress and a white tunic, and I'd swear you walked straight out of one of these exhibits!"

"Which is why I make a policy of never wearing head-dresses."

Michelle laughs, shaking her head. "I'll stay here with you for most of the morning, and then you can take over. Really your job until we get your mom's shipment and fit out the special exhibits room is to be accessible and help people have the best possible experience here you can. We have security on-site, so if there are ever any problems, you just call it in right away."

"Got it."

She fits me with a temporary name badge and a radio, and I hang out and try not to show how incredibly bored I am with the few dozen patrons who visit in the next two hours. I'm relieved when her radio buzzes and she leaves me with a smile and thumbs-up. It was starting to feel really pointless, standing in the corner.

But now I'm alone in a room with artifacts from my parents' heyday and a dead body that my father probably ushered into the afterlife. In the middle of San Diego, in America, where I was supposed to escape my history.

This is just phenomenally weird. I'm glad it's slow and no one has come through since Michelle left. I still can't stop smirking about kid-friendly Anubis. If they only knew.

"Hey!"

I about jump out of my skin and turn to see a lanky white girl grinning at me. She's nearly as tall as I am, with rectangle glasses and hair pulled back into a ponytail. Her button-down shirt and pin-striped black pants fit her awkwardly, pulled too tight across her shoulders and hips, like they weren't meant for her body. What if she has questions? I'm not going to pretend like Anubis is awesome, or try to get excited over the *amazing* stone-knife display. My mom's requirement is that I show up. I've done that.

"You're the new girl! Isadora, right? Michelle wasn't kidding—you look like you stepped out of one of the murals! Wow. That's so cool that you're actually Egyptian."

I paste a smile on my face. "Cool is one word for it."

"I'd kill for some sort of actual ethnic heritage. I'm a glorified mutt, really."

I frown. "Belonging to a specific race isn't the only way to have a culture. And being Egyptian doesn't make me *an* Egyptian."

She laughs, a sharp, barking laugh that explodes out of her stomach. I have never heard a laugh like it before. It's both alarming and disarming. "Yeah, gosh, you're right.

Sorry, I'm Tyler." She sticks out a hand that's narrow and bony. I shake it awkwardly because I know I'm supposed to. I still don't understand shaking hands.

"I'm working here over the summer for my aunt," she says.

"Who is your aunt?"

"Michelle."

I compare Tyler—pale, blond, lanky, tall Tyler—with tiny brunette Michelle. "Are you sure?"

"That's what my parents tell me. So, you wanna go get some lunch? I know an awesome taco stand a few blocks away. We may die of food poisoning, but it'll be a happy death."

"Are we allowed to leave?"

She waves a hand dismissively. "Yeah, no worries. I told Auntie Michelle."

I follow her out into the cloud-dimmed sunlight. She has a long, loping walk, her shoulders thrust forward and down, with her hands shoved into her pockets. Everything about her seems just off, just this side of awkward.

I officially give myself permission to like Tyler. She's been pressed into working for the museum, too. Liking her isn't giving my mother a victory. Besides, I can already tell it's going to be impossible *not* to like Tyler.

We walk under the arch and onto the bridge. I plan on spending future lunch breaks wandering around the park, getting to know the trees. There is a wealth of foliage, and

I'm shocked that everyone here doesn't have a permanent neck injury from craning to look at the trees at every possible chance. It boggles my mind how so much can grow. I thought this area was a desert, but it's nothing like the one I grew up in.

"This is great," I say, pausing to look over the side of the bridge and down into a shallow but steep-sided canyon. I'm nervous—I've never had to buy anything here, and though Sirus assures me that my plastic debit card is the same as money, I have no idea if it'll actually work. What if it doesn't? Then again, I need to figure the system out. The beginnings of a plot to drain my account of cash have been stirring in my head. If I have all the money out of the bank, Isis can't deny me access to it.

"Oh, sure. Nature is awesome." Tyler waves dismissively, leaning next to me to look down. Her face lights up. "Hey! HEY!"

I turn to stare at her, wondering why she's screaming. She waves her arms over her head. "HEY! RY! UP HERE!"

I follow her line of sight to a guy sitting in the curved hollow where two tree trunks meet, furiously scribbling in a black notebook. His hair is one shade away from midnight, worn a little long so that it curls just above his eyes. He's wearing khaki pants and a pale blue button-up short-sleeved shirt, showing off some seriously beautiful olive-toned arms. Wires dangle from earbuds and he hasn't looked up to see us yet.

"Boyfriend?" I ask. I hope she doesn't decide to have lunch with him instead. I definitely don't feel brave enough to go buy something on my own.

Tyler laughs. "No. In fact, I feel a little dirty because of my occasional lustful thoughts, since I'm taken. Still, I can appreciate beauty, right?" She leans forward, so far that I worry she'll lose her balance and topple right off the bridge. "Hey, RY!" Finally he looks up.

Floods, I have never seen such eyes.

They're crystal blue, a shade that shouldn't exist on the human body, a shade I immediately crave, a shade that makes my heart beat a little faster—almost as if I recognize it. I want to steal it, paint it, throw it into every room I ever decorate. It's the most perfect blue I've ever seen. Even from this distance his eyes are simply remarkable.

He pulls out his earbuds and smiles, a dimple on one side but not the other, though it looks like he's not quite focused on us, like his eyes are seeing just past us. He waves, and I have to admit Tyler is right about "appreciating beauty."

"What's up, Tyler?" His voice is a pleasant tenor.

"We're heading to lunch. Want to come?"

His eyes glance off me, again not quite focusing. Maybe he has bad vision, though I can see him just fine.

"Oh," Tyler shouts, "this is Isadora. She started at the

museum today. She's from Egypt!"

He looks back down at his notebook, tapping his pen against the page. "What part are you from?" he calls in flawless Arabic.

I narrow my eyes. Didn't see that one coming. "You wouldn't know it," I answer in English. He probably wants to show off that he speaks Arabic, but I don't like that he assumes I don't speak English well. I speak English perfectly. I speak *everything* perfectly.

He smiles, still not looking up, and Tyler finally leans back so I can stop worrying she'll fall over the side. "Coming or not?"

I hope he doesn't. If he does, I'll have to spend the whole time figuring out how to pull from his color scheme for a room. Black, brilliant blue, olive tan. And then the lips for an accent. Maybe the bedroom.

I blush. No bedrooms. Stupid. I should go back to the museum. I'm not even that hungry. Tyler clearly already has a social life and doesn't need me. I have no idea how to make friends.

"Rain check?" His eyes flit up and then back down, and relief floods through me. He makes me uncomfortable, and I don't know why.

"Sure. Later!"

Eyes still on his notebook, he waves at us.

I follow Tyler across the rest of the bridge. "Ry's great," she says. "We'll have to all hang out! You'll meet Scott, my boyfriend, sooner or later. He's a total nerd. Not as pretty as Ry, but fortunately for him I'm only mostly shallow."

I shrug and smile. Doesn't matter to me whether her boyfriend is as pretty as Ry. I don't care about Ry. But that doesn't stop me from obsessively re-creating his eyes in my memory, and trying to figure out if there's any sort of non-crazy way to take a picture of him.

Just for the color palette.

I try to balance the cow-horn headdress, though my head still isn't big enough for it and it keeps slipping down over my eyes. I'll bet when I'm eleven it will fit.

I hold it on, looking at myself in the burnished copper of my mother's mirror. In the blurred image that stares back at me, I can almost see myself as her, and it makes me feel pretty. I wonder what I'll be the goddess of when I'm old enough for it. I think I'd like to be the goddess of animals. Maybe then Ubesti would purr more for me.

I stand, walking around the room with my back as straight as I can make it, holding the headdress and staring solemnly ahead.

"What are you doing?" a voice snaps, and I jump, startled into letting go of the headdress, which clatters to the ground.

"I was just—hi, Hathor. I was just . . . umm." I blush, humiliated. My brother Horus and his wife, Hathor, are visiting, and even though he's my brother he feels more like an uncle, because he's old. Hathor is beautiful, but in a different way than Mother. Mother's beauty is warm and safe. Hathor's makes me feel small and ugly.

"That's mine," she hisses.

"No! I would never take anything of yours! It's my mother's."

"Stupid girl. Your mother is the one who took it in the first place. It was mine. It is mine. I will never forget what Isis took from me." She leans over and picks it up by the horns, the single polished disc of gold between the horns gleaming dully in the lantern light. "Mine," she whispers, placing it on her own head, and I stumble back. Seeing it on her head makes me realize how stupid I must have looked, trying to wear it.

"Hathor," my mother's voice says, in the angry tone that gives me a headache. I turn around, waiting to get in trouble, but where my mother should be standing in the doorway is nothing but an outline, darkness blacker than night, emptier than the desert sky.

I close my eyes. I don't want to see it. It shouldn't be there, and I don't want it to see me, either.

Set murdered Osiris. Isis and Nephthys brought Osiris back from the dead, but once dead, he remained god of the underworld.

Set killed Horus. Isis used magic from Thoth to revive him.

Isis poisoned Amun-Re, only healing him once he divulged his true name and gave her and Horus power over him.

Horus used that power to defeat Set and become pharaoh-god of Egypt.

Nephthys wanted a child. Set was unable or unwilling to give her one, so she disguised herself as the more beautiful Isis and seduced Osiris.

Set and Osiris get together once a week to play board games.

"WHAT ARE YOU DOING?" I STARE AT SIRUS IN horror. He's sitting at the table, eyes closed, mouth moving as he whispers to himself. And in front of him, in a notebook, he's writing glyphs for the names of our parents.

He finishes, then looks at me and shrugs. "Remembering."

"You still pray? You *pray* to our parents?" I can't keep

the disgust out of my voice. "You actually worship them. Floods, Sirus, what is wrong with you?"

"I'm not worshipping. I'm remembering."

"The way Isis forced you to!"

"You would rather I pretend like I have no heritage? Pretend like I came from nowhere, from nothing? A lot of cultures revere their ancestors, Isadora. It's not worship. It's respect, and gratitude."

"It's sick! It's the only reason they had us! You're giving them exactly what they want."

He stands, picking up the notebook. "You have the relationship with Mom and Dad that you choose to. Please don't criticize mine."

My jaw hangs open as he walks past me out of the room. I thought coming here would mean leaving all of that behind, but apparently Sirus brought it right along with him. I turn and startle at movement, until I realize it's just my reflection in a mirror hanging on the wall.

For a moment I thought it was my mother.

My reflection smiles as an idea takes root. I pull at my hair, thick and long like Isis's. She *loves* my hair.

My smiles grows.

"Are you sure?" Amberlyn looks at me dubiously. A massive cloth flower clip takes up half of her head. It's magenta and leopard print, with a plastic eyeball in the middle. I knew she was the right girl for the job the second I laid eyes on that.

"Absolutely."

"Okay. Because I think we can rock this, I really do, but I want you to be sure. I hate it when girls tell me they want this and then cry."

"Hack it off." I glare at myself in the mirror. No more "Gosh, you look like you could be on a mural!" comments at the museum. Ever. One week of them was enough for a lifetime. I'm not part of that exhibit, and I never will be.

I hate today. Last night I broke down and emailed Isis, just to make sure she was doing okay, even though I swore to myself I wouldn't. Of course she emailed back, and I got it right after the weird fight thing with Sirus.

> Little Heart,
>
> I miss you, too. Try to make some friends. Stop eating so much sugar.
>
> I caught Hathor in my workroom during their last visit; we were right not to send you to Horus. The dreams have continued unabated, though you are no longer threatened in them, which is a great comfort and relief. Are you still having them?
>
> Nephthys is here to help me prepare for the baby and assist on charms to combat the dark forces at work. Your father sends his love. Don't worry about us.
>
> Love,
>
> Your Mother
>
> P.S. I mean it about the sugar.

I pop a sucker back into my mouth, making sure to trace the sugar-on-a-stick around all of my teeth. Just remembering her email makes me seethe. "*I miss you, too.*" I didn't *say* I missed her, and I'm sure she doesn't miss me. And that part about my father sending his love? What love? I doubt he's even noticed I'm gone.

And any bad dreams I've had are no doubt a result of my brain trying to process my stupid childhood. Once things settle down and I really feel like I have a life outside of all of that, I'm sure my brain will quit rehashing weird childhood memories.

I take a deep breath and narrow my eyes at the mirror. I should send Isis a picture when it's finished. She'll have a heart attack. A grin spreads across my face as Amberlyn grabs a section near the front and spreads the goop on it, then wraps it in foil.

An hour and a half later Amberlyn spins me around, looking nervous.

I laugh. My black hair is shorter than it's been since I was a baby, a pixie cut styled in a feminine version of the fauxhawk. And near the front is a chunk dyed hunter green.

"It's perfect!" With my black-lined eyes, deep-purple tank top, and dark jeans, I look tough. I look interesting. And I look *nothing* like my mother.

Amberlyn lets out a relieved breath and gives me detailed instructions on how to take care of it so the color lasts longer. I happily pay her; before I came I looked up the customs for paying stylists, so I leave an eighty-percent tip. The fact that my mother paid for what she will consider an absolute butchery is icing on the cake. Who misses who now?

I grab Deena's bike and walk it down the sidewalk, the day warm in spite of the clouds that won't go away. San Diego's hills have quickly made me repent of my initial excitement over this form of transportation. Who designed this city? It's a good thing Sirus is around to take me to work and bring me home. I'd probably die if I had to pedal everywhere.

I pause, watching someone use an ATM. Interesting. The card goes in, but instead of magically paying for something, actual money comes out. . . . Looks like I have something new to research when I get home.

A smoothie shop on the corner of a brown, tired-looking strip mall calls to me, and I ditch my bike against a lamppost. It smells heavenly inside, all citrus and sugar. I order some strawberry-mango-banana concoction that's heavy on the sherbet. As I walk outside, I sincerely hope it will give me a cavity. I've never had dental problems before, and even though I can't quit flossing and brushing three times a day (I've tried, but the residual Isis guilt gives me a headache), maybe a massive influx of sugar will do the trick.

The nearest green plastic table is occupied by a guy

hunched over a notebook, so I take the free one next to him and give myself a brain freeze. The only thing that could make this moment better would be if the clouds would go away. I'd love to feel the sun on my day off, and I haven't once seen the stars. It's starting to make me twitchy, disconnected. Maybe tonight will be clear.

"Isadora?"

I jump, knocking over my smoothie. "Floods!" I mutter, flipping it back up and resealing the lid. A lump of the frozen pink drink is slowly spreading out along my table. I look up to see the culprit and am met by a pair of perfectly blue eyes. Ry.

He's staring at me like he's seen a ghost. Even his olive skin has paled. After a few seconds he shakes his head, coming back to himself. "Sorry! I didn't mean to startle you." He grabs his stack of napkins and sops up the mess.

"It's not a big deal. Don't worry about it."

He finishes cleaning anyway, dumping the napkins in the trash right next to me and then grabbing his bag and sitting down at my table.

"Your hair. I didn't recognize you before."

I lift a finger self-consciously to my chopped locks. "Oh, yeah. You have a good memory."

"No, I mean, I didn't recognize you when we met before. But now I do."

I frown. "Umm, what?" Why would he have recognized me before? I doubt he's spent any summers in Abydos.

"Sorry." He smiles, his teeth big and white and very straight. "I mean, of course I remember you. I remember interesting faces."

"Interesting? Wow. That's flattering."

He laughs. "You have perfect, classic features. I like it. You don't look like everyone else here."

"Lucky me?" I take a long draw on my straw, not sure what we're supposed to talk about now. It's not like we're friends. I don't even know Ry. Why did he sit with me?

He keeps staring, this strange expression on his face. Finally, his beautiful lips once again parting in a smile like he knows a joke I don't, he pulls his pen from behind his ear and goes back to the tattered black notebook. He starts scribbling away like I'm not even here. Which, yet again, begs the question of why he sat here in the first place.

"Sorry," he says, not looking up. "Just gotta get this description down before I lose it. Suddenly I have a deadline."

"Sure." I have no idea what he's talking about, but I'm drinking my smoothie so fast my throat feels like it's caked in ice. The sooner I finish, the sooner I have two hands to steer my bike. He's too handsome. That's what it is. He's too handsome, and the way he has his shoulders thrown back, the way that grin slowly splits apart his face, the way it tells you that everything is funny to him and always will be because he is so pretty he can laugh at anything and get away with it, yes, all of that,

that is what I will not like about him.

I don't know why I have such an itching need to invent reasons to dislike him. But it's important. I can feel a strange something budding inside of me. I refuse to let it take root.

And he's still writing in his stupid notebook. He's *rude* and arrogant. And I don't like the way one of his curls flops down on his forehead. It's stupid. I want to push it off, back into the rest of his hair.

No I don't. I don't want to touch him. I don't care to find out if his hair is as soft as it looks. Why can't I drink this smoothie faster?

"Okay." He sets his pen down emphatically and looks up at me with a smile. "I always have to write these things when I think of them. Even if it turns out to be crap later, you never know, right?"

"Umm, yeah."

He waits for a few seconds. "You aren't going to ask me what I'm writing, are you?"

I shrug. "Nope."

"I like that. I like your hair, too. The green is a nice contrast."

"Wanted something different."

"I declare it a success."

I roll my eyes. "My life is complete." I take a few last desperate gulps while he sits there, leaning back, completely at ease, watching me with that infuriating secret smile. He's probably always this secure. Is he trying to flirt with me? I have no idea. When I'd go out on the rare excursion with my mother, it was easy enough to brush off any hopeful flirters by pretending I didn't speak Arabic. (Though often as not they were trying to flirt with my mother, too. Blech.)

Unfortunately, I can't pretend like I don't speak English with Ry.

"Well, nice seeing you again." I stand and, to my chagrin, he does too.

"What are you doing?"

"Throwing away this empty cup."

He laughs. He does that a lot. "I mean, today. Let me show you around. I am a living Google Map when it comes to the best restaurants in San Diego."

"So is that what's in the notebook? Restaurant reviews and maps?"

He laughs again. He tips his head back and his throat moves in this interesting way. I'll bet he practices in front of the mirror. "Nope. Maybe the next notebook. But have you been to the harbor yet? There's a genuinely terrifying sculpture that you have to see to believe."

"Thanks, but I have my bike. Gotta get it back."

"Not a problem!" He points to the parking lot, where a truck sits. Not just any truck. A fully restored truck straight out of the 1950s, painted sky blue with a white stripe, bursting with personality that modern trucks only wish they had. It is twenty different kinds of awesome.

"Floods," I whisper under my breath.

"What?"

I shake my head. "Sorry, I'm just crushing on your truck." He beams and I inwardly cringe. Why did I admit that?

"She's pretty great, isn't she?"

I pick up my bike. This has gotten off track. I don't know why he's so eager to hang out with me today. And I don't care. I have no interest in boys, now or ever. I can't help but notice him, and—oh, idiot gods, I am *definitely* attracted to him. This is how it starts. This is how I set myself up for pain and tragedy and endings where I want eternities.

I refuse. I refuse it all. I will never attach myself to someone else. I can end everything before it starts and be free and alone and perfectly happy.

"Maybe another time. My brother's waiting for me."

"Can I give you a ride home?"

"Sorry, my mother told me never to accept rides from strangers." Not true; it was never an issue. I was never far enough away from her as a child for her to worry. But it was something she *would* say to me. Hmm . . . actually, I'm glad she never said it to me, because if she had, I'd be forced to ride with him just to go against her.

"I'll have to work on being less strange, then. It was good to finally see you." That secret smile again. I want to smoosh his cheeks together to get rid of it.

I wave, climbing onto my bike and peddling away. At the corner light I risk a glance back to see if he's watching me. He's sitting, scribbling madly in his notebook. Good. I didn't want him to be watching me.

Boys suck.

Even when they have perfect blue eyes and ridiculously cool trucks. Maybe especially then.

I punch in the code to the garage, dumping my bike against the wall. Blue, blue, blue. I need to get that color out of my system. I'll figure out where to—

I pause, halfway through the door from the garage to the laundry room.

Something is wrong.

The now-bare skin at the back of my neck prickles as I stare into the empty house. Sirus is on an LA drive today. Deena is still at work.

I breathe in deeply, and there, again—something is wrong. Their house always smells vaguely of Tide detergent and the cold salt of the sea, but there's too much salt now. Salt and . . . chlorine?

Maybe they had someone here cleaning the pool today and didn't tell me.

I walk forward, silently, cautiously. Through the kitchen and into the dining room, where something crunches underfoot. Glass—hundreds of shards of glass.

A breeze cuts across me and I look up to see that the sliding glass door to the patio and pool is smashed out, gaping and jagged and open.

Every sense on alert, I slowly retreat into the kitchen and slide a long, serrated knife out of the block on the counter. Keeping my back to the wall, I creep past the dining room, into the family room. Everything seems in order. TV and electronics still where they ought to be—even Deena's sleek laptop, just sitting there on the couch.

I keep going, the only noise wind chimes drifting in from the patio, their cheerful notes at odds with the electric atmosphere inside. I stop dead when I come to the entry.

The front door is wide open.

I know—I *know*—it was closed when I pulled up on my bike not two minutes ago. Whoever was here is gone.

Or maybe they aren't. I look up the stairs, only half a flight visible before it turns around a sharp corner. Clutching the knife, I walk up the stairs, each step measured and silent. If they are still here, they know I am, too, because the garage door opened. Hopefully they heard that and ran. But if not . . .

My breaths come fast, my heartbeat racing. I make it to the landing at the top of the stairs, the second-story hall stretching out in front of me. The first door on my right is already open. I peek around the doorframe and then whip my head back so I can process what I saw. Empty. This

74

is the room that'll be the baby's, and there's nothing in it but a scattering of paint-sample squares and some empty boxes.

The next door is a closet. I open it, cringing at the squeaky hinges, and stab inward with the knife.

Nothing.

Three more rooms. The bathroom, my room, and the master bedroom. The bathroom is easily cleared—thankfully they have a glass shower door rather than a curtain. I creep across the hall to my room, painfully aware of how loud doorknobs click if you don't open them slowly. I push the door, and—

Floods.

The drawers have been pulled out of the dresser and thrown everywhere. There's a dent in the wall above where one lies smashed and broken on the floor. My clothes are strewn madly about the room. A notebook I had for writing down design ideas has been torn apart, individual sheets scattered among the clothes.

My suitcase is in the middle of the room, literally ripped open, the pockets sliced and gaping like wounds. My closet door hangs wide open, everything flung out. The whole room smells like the weird combination of scents downstairs, magnified.

I take one step in and hear more glass cracking underfoot. I lean down to pick up the only picture I brought—a framed shot of my mother and me, on the banks of the

Nile, when I was ten. I'd left it in my suitcase, along with the amulets she forced me to bring. Those, too, are under-foot, each snapped in half.

I don't—I can't even—what? Why?

There's a noise from downstairs and I whip around, brandishing the knife.

"Isadora?" Sirus calls, fear in his voice. "Isadora? Are you home?"

Letting out a breath I've been holding for far too long, I close my bedroom door and answer him.

Deena's still out on the driveway talking with the police officers. While she found time between cataloging the house for any missing items and watching the police dust for prints to tell me she loves my hair, somehow I don't think it made the right impression on the law-enforcement end of things. I was interviewed four times, most of the questions revolving around whether I knew anyone who might have done this.

I know a grand total of three people here that I'm not related to, and somehow I doubt Tyler is the smash-glass-doors-and-destroy-rooms type.

"Why didn't you call the police?" Sirus asks, shaking his head as I hold the dustpan for the shards of glass. No prints anywhere; all that's left now is cleaning up the mess.

"Didn't think of it."

"Honestly, Isadora, you don't live in the middle of the

desert with a bunch of gods anymore. There are a lot of dangerous people around. You should have left the house immediately."

He's right, of course. It never crossed my mind.

"If something had happened to you . . . I'm just so glad no one was home."

"Do they think it's someone with a grudge against Deena?" She knows most of the officers who showed up, and she works for the government, after all.

"She's never been in criminal prosecuting. The loonies she deals with are usually rich, entitled loonies. They're the suing type, not the violent type."

He still looks uneasy. We all are. Knowing it was that simple for someone to come into the house? Everything feels different now.

The front door closes, and then Deena walks in and leans against the wall, surveying the broken door with an exhausted expression, hand absently rubbing her stomach. "They think it was someone looking for prescription drugs. You must have scared him off before he could get through all the rooms."

"I am the scariest," I say, dumping another load of shards into the trash with a discordant tinkling.

"I'll take over here," she says. "When we're done with the glass and get something taped up over the door, I'll help with your room."

"It's okay. It's my stuff, I'll clean it up."

"I'm so sorry. Nothing like this has ever happened before."

"It's not your fault," I say. "Just random, right?" But it *feels* personal. It feels like chaos caught up to me and let me know it's here with a vengeance.

I walk up the stairs and stand on the threshold of my room, staring at the destruction, and I can't help but shiver, putting my hand on the back of my neck. I pick up the photo in its frame. The crack in the glass runs right between my mother and me.

|||
|||

In the history of mythology in ancient Egypt, Isis is not only the mother of Horus, she's also occasionally his wife. While deeply disturbing to me, this has less to do with actual relationships and more to do with the balance of power and worship. As Hathor fell out of favor, my mother gladly stepped in and usurped her followers, thereby taking her roles, her domains, and even her husband.

Eventually the gods settled into their most commonly worshipped forms—in this case, Isis as mother and not wife, and Hathor as very annoyed wife, still angry over the loss of her worshippers and favorite cow-horned headdress.

Isis has never apologized. More followers meant more worship, more tongues whispering her name, more hearts turned toward her in times of crisis. To a member of a constantly shifting pantheon of gods desperate for relevance, this was worth occasionally stepping in as the ceremonial wife of her favorite son.

Worship is everything.

But seriously, gross.

TUESDAY AFTER FRIDAY'S BREAK-IN IS THE FIRST time I've been home alone since then. I wait on the curb in front of Sirus's house. An unfamiliar car pulls up with an older woman in the driver's seat. Tyler leans over and waves at me from the passenger seat, so I climb into the back.

"Thank you so much for the ride," I say. "Sirus is stuck at the airport with a delayed flight. You saved me." I've actually been out here waiting for an hour. The back door is replaced and a security system installed, but it still feels creepy in there alone.

"No problem! You can thank my mother, Julie. Or as I like to call her while my clunker's in the shop, my personal chauffeur."

Julie's just a bit smaller than Tyler, and I realize why all Tyler's nice clothes look like they were made to fit someone else: they actually were. Her voice sounds almost the same as her daughter's. "If you keep referring to me as your chauffeur, I'm going to start charging you."

"Volunteering does make me the big bucks. It's about time I started helping out around here. Do you prefer imaginary checks, or imaginary credit cards?"

"I take nonimaginary dish washing."

"Oh, sorry. I'm afraid my dish-washing account got closed for overdrafting."

They laugh, teasing each other back and forth, and it feels so easy and comfortable. Which for some reason makes me *un*comfortable.

"So, Isadora. Tyler tells me you're from Egypt?"

"Born and raised."

"Do you miss it?"

"Just the desert. And the quiet. There are a *lot* of people here."

"That's the downside to San Diego. Once you live here, you never want to live anywhere else. Unfortunately everyone else already lives here." She smiles at me in the rearview mirror. "Would you like to come for dinner sometime?"

"I'd love to." I want to know more about Tyler, see what made her as awesome as she is. She's the best part about working at the museum, and I greedily want to have her in more parts of my life here.

Tyler holds back a closed fist and it only takes me a few seconds to remember I'm supposed to bump it with my own. "Sweet," she says. "This means we'll actually have to make dinner for once, though."

"We'll do something Middle Eastern to make you feel at home," Tyler's mom says. I smile, but what they have feels nothing like my home. And it makes me sad.

When she drops us off, Tyler and I have to practically shove our way into the lobby. It's the third Tuesday of the month, so the museum is free to San Diego residents. Michelle had mentioned this before, but I had no idea just how seriously San Diegans take Free Museum Day. It's packed. Tyler and I are working the front desks together, checking IDs. I'm grateful I'm not upstairs—at least I don't have to worry about watching this many people in the exhibit, or, heaven forbid, the Children's Discovery Room.

I haven't slept well since the break-in. I can't get the smell out of my room, and it's giving me constant headaches. This press of people isn't helping the pain.

My headache reminds me of last night's new email from my mother, whom I always associate with pain in my temples. She informed me there is a fifty-dollar-a-day withdrawal limit on my debit card. I hadn't even taken any money out yet. I'd only started plotting to do it when I had somewhere to go, somewhere she couldn't find me.

How did she know? *How does she always know?*

"Are you okay?" Tyler shouts from the other side of the lobby.

I wave a couple through after they show me their driver's licenses. "I'm peachy," I say over the crowd. "Why?"

She shrugs. "I don't know. You seem . . . tired."

A tall guy, late teens, wearing aviator sunglasses and jeans that hang so low on his hips it's a miracle of gravity they stay on, stands right in front of me. "Hey," he says with a half grin that I assume is supposed to be sexy but really looks like he has poor facial-muscle control. "What's your name?"

"San Diego County driver's license or pay at the front desk," I snap. Looking confused, he pulls out his wallet and drops it on the ground. He swears, picks it back up, and walks to a group of friends all snickering in the doorway.

Tyler laughs. "Okay, you don't look tired. You look angry."

"I look angry?"

"Only when guys try to hit on you. But you totally work it. You kind of rock angry. If I tried to be angry, I'd just look like I was constipated or something."

I shake my head but can't hold back a smile. "Well, good to know that if I'm unpleasant, at least I look good doing it."

"Exactly! The rest of us are forced to be nice by our inferior looks."

"Oh, shut up." But now I'm really grinning. Tyler has that effect on people.

I feel someone's eyes on me, and I turn, catching a fleeting glimpse of a very tall, dark figure as he turns the corner and goes up the stairs. Not the sunglasses idiot from before, but some familiarity nags at me even though I didn't really see him.

A woman's already waiting with an ID in front of me. I don't have time to run down someone who may or may not have been creeping around. We probably just forgot to check his ID. Understandable in this crush of people.

When will I stop being so nervous and edgy? Last night when I was coming out of the bathroom, Sirus surprised me and I nearly tackled him before I realized he wasn't some shadowy attacker.

I shake it off as a short, barrel-chested guy wearing a

graphic T-shirt and khaki shorts walks in and folds his arms, glaring as groups of people move in and out around him. His black hair is deliberately messy, and he has chunky glasses. "What does a guy have to do to get some service?"

Tyler sees him and scowls. "Look, kid, the Children's Discovery Room closed five minutes ago. You're just gonna have to go to the park."

"The only parking I do is with my girlfriend." His face breaks into a goofy smile and Tyler laughs her horsey laugh, smacking him in the shoulder as he envelops her in a hug. His nose hits at her chin, and they are such a painfully awkward couple, I think it might be the cutest thing I've ever seen.

The brutality of being temporary hits me like a sandstorm, leaving me raw. They love each other right now, but right now is all they'll have. We aren't made for forever, and neither are our relationships.

Scott (at least I'm assuming this is the elusive Scott; otherwise Tyler has some explaining to do) pretends to bite her neck and then kisses her cheek. "Late lunch/early dinner?"

"We're off soon." Tyler turns him around and points at me. "That's Isadora."

"Ah, the mystical Isadora." Scott grins and waves at me. "She *is* tall and scary pretty. You were right. Coming to eat with us?"

I shrug. "I—"

"Of course she is." Tyler shoves him to the side. "Now go play. Some of us are working."

"Scary?" I raise an eyebrow at her.

"Scary *pretty*. *Scary* is the modifier, not the descriptor."

After twenty minutes our relief finally comes, and Tyler and I stumble out into the brilliant sunshine, done for the day. I take a deep breath, glad to be free of that madhouse. Being around huge groups of people is still weird for me. We took the occasional trip to Cairo and other cities around Egypt, but for the most part my childhood was practically sequestered. It's like they were grooming me to be a shut-in or something.

I'm looking forward to when my mom's shipment of stuff gets here. It was held up in customs, so I've been doing regular museum work. At least when all of her crap arrives, I'll be able to organize and arrange it instead of checking IDs or standing in the Egyptian room and trying to look so aloof and intimidating that people won't ask me questions and local college guys will quit trying to pick me up.

I rub my eyes, unused to the brightness after being inside for several hours. But then it hits me—the sunshine! The clouds burned off early today! I tip my head back and close my eyes, luxuriating in the sensation of the sun on my skin.

"There they are," Tyler says, pulling my arm. I turn and see Scott, lounging on the steps to the side of the museum, talking animatedly with . . . Ry. Who is nodding and smiling but still scribbling in his notebook. I haven't seen him since that ridiculous encounter at the smoothie place.

"You guys!" Tyler points one long arm straight up. "The *sun*!"

"Is that what the strange ball of brilliant light and heat in the place of my beloved clouds is?" Scott asks, scratching his head.

"And do you know what that means?" Tyler prods.

"The crops will grow, the children will sing, and the land will rejoice?" I offer.

"Yes! Also, my skin will burn. Burn, burn, burn. And if I'm going to get a sunburn, I'm going to do it at the beach. Let's go."

I'd planned on hanging out in the park for a couple of hours before Sirus picks me up. I'm in a black faux-leather pencil skirt and a cerulean-blue tank blouse. And my gladiator sandals? Not exactly beachwear.

"I've got clothes in Scott's car. You can borrow some of my stuff," Tyler says, reading my mind.

"I don't know; I was going to hang out here." I wonder if Ry is going. And if he is, whether that makes me want to more, or less. Probably less. He still hasn't looked up from his scribbling.

"Oh, come on!" Tyler throws her arm around me. "Have you even been to the beach yet?"

"I rode past it a couple of times, and—"

"Ha! No! You are still an ocean virgin, and today you lose your virginity!"

"I have the weirdest girlfriend alive," Scott muses, staring up at the sky.

Tyler's arm locks me into place. "No arguments. You've been here two weeks, and all you ever do is work and go home. Come to the beach with us! We'll get pizza, and play Mock the Worst-Fitting Swimwear, and we can watch the sunset. The sunsets are amazing, and the stars over the ocean—"

"Stars?" I perk up. She's right! If the clouds burned off this early, maybe the stars will be out tonight.

"Yes! Oh, good. I'm so glad you're coming!" She steers me down the stairs and through a geometric garden, all shaped planters and yellow-and-blue-tiled fountains, to the parking lot. She takes a deep breath and spews out a series of sentences so fast it's only after she's in a car with the door locked that I realize she said, "There's not enough room in Scotty's car for all of us, so you'll ride with Ry, okay? See you there!" Scott's in, too, and they pull out like they're fleeing the law.

I turn to see Ry standing right next to me, smiling. "Riding with me then? Great!"

Floods. *Did Tyler just set me up?*

If only his truck weren't so beautiful. I lean my head back and close my eyes, letting the breeze from the open window play across my face. Amun-Re, I love this truck.

"So, how do you like San Diego?" he asks, more or less, since he says it in fluent Arabic, complete with Egyptian accent. He's tapping on the steering wheel, eyes straight ahead on the road, but a dimple hints that he wants to smile that stupid smile and it's all he can do not to.

I'm tempted to answer him in Urdu, but I opt for English instead. "It's fine." Other than creepy drug-addict prowlers who destroy my personal property. "Why do you keep trying to speak to me in Arabic?"

"I don't know, I thought maybe you were homesick."

"Trust me, not homesick. Sick of home. Which is why I'm here." He's a show-off, that's what he is. I don't give a mummified cat whether or not he can speak Arabic. I add *show-off* to my list of reasons why I will never like Ry in a way that would be dangerous. And then I'm mad that I even feel like I need to have a list, which is another thing to put on the list I wish I didn't have to have.

"So, I'm not strange anymore?" he asks.

"What?"

"You're riding in my car, which must mean I'm not a stranger anymore."

"Actually, the more I'm around you, the stranger you get."

Ry laughs, but his phone buzzes and he pulls it out. "Yeah? No parking at all? Sure, let's meet there. Not a problem. Bye."

He turns off of the main road. We weave down the hills, teasing glimpses of the ocean blinding me. It still shocks me every time I come over a hill and see it spreading out on the horizon. It feels wrong, that much water. My eyes keep trying to turn it into sand, heat shimmers, something that makes sense.

I don't recognize this neighborhood—the homes are close together but big. Here they cram as much house onto as little land as they possibly can. Cars are parked all down the narrow street, and guys carrying surfboards walk barefoot on the asphalt.

There's no space in this city. Anywhere. I want open land. I want desert. I want to be able to look in a single direction and see *nothing*.

Crap. I am not homesick. I'm not, I'm not.

Ry slows and I see Scott's car (the color of puke mating with rust) pulling up into the driveway of a massive home, complete with huge Grecian pillars and a fountain. The whole thing is so ostentatious it borders on laughable. Okay, I do laugh a little bit.

"Can we park here?" I ask.

"It's okay, we know the owners."

I shake my head at the monstrosity of a house. "Do you know the architects? Because they should be shot."

"You know, I kinda agree." His mouth twists into that smile again, and it sets my teeth on edge. He always seems to be in his own little world, his blue eyes never quite focused on this one except for that brief time with the smoothies. Not that I want them focused on me, but still.

Ry pulls in behind Scott. Tyler's already out of the car, grabbing towels and a big canvas bag out of the trunk. "You boys get the pizza and meet us there. Okay, Isadora, you want the daisy bikini, or the pink one?"

Who is this girl and how did I end up here?

Thirty minutes later we're on the sand by ourselves. Or, well, by ourselves and about 400 billion other people. Thankfully Tyler had a black cover-up for this painfully pastel bikini I'm wearing. It only took me seven minutes to text Sirus that I don't need a ride home—I'm getting better. He texts me back and reminds me about the new security system. It's an unnecessary reminder. I spent all the hours I couldn't sleep last night reading the manual and memorizing how it works.

Tyler stretches her legs over the edge of the huge towel and digs her toes into the sand, leaning back onto her elbows. "If the boys don't get back with our pizza in the next five minutes, I will die of starvation."

"Scott seems nice," I say, watching the water warily. I want a bank on the other side. And no waves. Then I'd like it.

Tyler smiles, watching the water happily. "He is. He's

90

also a huge, huge dork. I love him. But seriously, if he's not back soon, it's over. I will propose to the next boy who walks by with anything edible."

"Fickle woman," Scott says from behind us, setting down a pizza box with a flourish. Ry puts another on top of it and hands me a bottle of Coke.

Oh, glorious, glorious caffeine and sugar. I can make it through anything as long as I have enough of those two. My mother never let me have soda. I've had as much as I possibly can since I got here. She's right—I'm addicted, and it gives me headaches, and I don't care. "Thanks. How much do I owe you?"

He waves a hand dismissively and plops onto the sand next to me. "Nothing; don't worry about it."

I frown. "I'm paying you back."

"Pick up the tab next time."

What does he mean by "next time"? Does he think this will be a regular thing? It doesn't sound very datey, though, because aren't American boys supposed to pay for girls all the time?

Floods. This is stupid. Free food is free food. I take a long drink and then help myself to a slice piled high with mounds of vegetables. The cheese is thick, the crust just barely sturdy enough not to collapse under the weight of the toppings. I've had pizza a couple of times, but this is the best yet.

Scott shudders, pulling a plain cheese slice out of the

other box. "How can you eat all that? It's so polluted. You've gotten away from the purity of the perfect blend of sauce, bread, and cheese."

I take another massive bite and shrug. "It's more interesting. This is the best pizza I've ever had."

Ry beams. "Told you I was a restaurant Google Map. You should have trusted me."

"Noted," I say, unable to avoid smiling.

Scott is still staring at my slice in agitation. "But— the onions! Just the thought of biting into them . . ." He shudders.

"I can eat onions like apples," I say.

"Shut up," Tyler says.

"I ate them all the time growing up. It's no big deal." Ancient Egyptians were big into onions, and my mother never really got past it. Doesn't give you the nicest breath, but they add just the right amount of flavor and texture to nearly anything. Few dishes can't be improved by the liberal addition of onions, as far as I'm concerned. Isis used to chop them so finely it was how I imagined snow would look.

"That's the most disgusting thing I've ever heard." Scott's eyes are wide with both admiration and horror.

I pull off a big chunk of purple onion and stick it on my tongue, slowly pulling it into my mouth and chewing, channeling Hathor.

Tyler laughs. "Sexy!"

"Don't even think about trying that," Scott says. "I

refuse to kiss you if you've been eating onions."

"Like you could resist!" Tyler finishes her cheese and grabs a slice of the veggie, eyebrows raised defiantly.

"You're a terrible influence on my girlfriend." Scott pouts as the onion-covered slice disappears into Tyler's mouth. "Ry, tell them that's disgusting."

We all look over at Ry to find him chewing absently on his pizza while writing in one of his notebooks. Of course. What a weirdo.

He continues to write in the notebook while we swim. Anyone who says the water is great in San Diego really means the water feels like it was imported directly from the Arctic. The waves freak me out, but I remind myself about their biggest perk: no hippos.

We finish the rest of the pizza and enjoy a rousing round of Mock the Worst-Fitting Swimwear. Not even the grand prize winner, a nine-months-pregnant woman in a string bikini, gets so much as a glance from Notebook Boy.

I don't understand why Scott and Tyler like having him around. There's no point. He's like furniture or something. Really pretty furniture, but still.

A volleyball smashes into the sand next to me, and I look up to find two guys in low-slung board shorts grinning sheepishly. "Hey, sorry about that. You want to play?"

"No, thanks."

"Aw, come on!"

"Again, no thanks." I don't even bother picking up the ball to throw it at them, and they walk away, grumbling.

"Ooh, they had pretty abs. You should have said yes," Tyler says.

"Bodies are bodies. Who cares."

"Speaking of bodies," Scott says, his head resting on Tyler's stomach. "Bruce Lee could have taken Chuck Norris in their prime, and you know it."

I have no idea who they're talking about. I'm tracing patterns in the sand with my toes, warily watching the horizon as the sun sinks. No clouds yet. Please, no clouds.

Tyler shoves his head away. "Could not! Ry, tell him he's wrong."

Ry holds up a finger and we wait while he writes . . . and writes . . . and writes. Tyler and Scott giggle, just watching him, like it's a game to see how long he'll go. Knowing those two, it probably *is* a game. And finally, two full minutes later with the sun nearly setting, he sets down his pen and folds the notebook shut. "What are we talking about?"

"Now, or any time in the last three hours?" I snap, surprised at how pissed I sound. What do I care if he hangs out and ignores us?

He smiles, looking right into my eyes, and my breath catches as I see that he is here, finally, connected to me and only me. "Now."

"You'll have to excuse Ry," Scott says. "He's a poet."

"Here we go." Ry rolls his eyes, breaking the connection, and I feel like I can breathe again.

"Ask him what type of poetry he writes." Scott's face twists up in a smirk. Tyler reaches past me and pats Ry's leg supportively.

"What type of poetry do you write?" I say, my voice flat.

"Epic!" Scott shouts. "He writes epic poetry!"

Ry shrugs. "It's true."

"Epic poetry? What does that mean?"

He tucks the notebook into his bag and turns to look at me again, and I swear his eyes are like a physical blow, they're so shockingly beautiful, and I wish he'd look somewhere else. "Really, really long? And with specific conventions. Starts in the middle of a story; there's always a quest; really strict meter; you have to invoke a muse. In my case Calliope. It's kind of along the lines of *The Iliad*. You know it?"

"Of course. I used to read it under the covers at night on my laptop."

Everyone gives me weird looks. "Why?" Tyler asks.

"Oh, my mom kind of has this thing against the Greeks."

"Seriously?"

"Yup. Not a fan. So I had to sneak around to read *The Iliad* and *The Odyssey*."

"I thought my mom was weird for banning vampire novels," Tyler says. "Don't tell her you're hanging out with Ry, then."

"Why?"

"Full-blooded Greek." He smiles at me with that dimple and that skin, and it's too perfect. Is there something wrong with me that I want to hang out with him more just because he's Greek and it'd kill my mom?

Tyler whispers something to Scott, and they both jump up. "Be right back!" she says, and they take off down the beach, hand in hand.

"They're going somewhere to make out, aren't they?" I ask, frowning at them.

"Probably."

"Lame."

Ry and I sit there, staring out over the ocean as the sun's dipping progress speeds up. I make a point of keeping my eyes on the water. It glows now, this brilliant, darkening blue. It's amazing. I should come here for sunset every night. I don't wish away the water anymore.

"So," I say, too aware of him right next to me and wanting to talk about something normal, "why epic poetry?"

"I know there's no point—not like anyone wants to read it—but I grew up on these stories, the mythology, and it's a beautiful way of making sense of the world. Plus I have high hopes that my poetry will get me the one thing I want in the whole world." He lets that hang there, like he wants me to ask what it is.

Instead I say, "Doesn't everyone always meet really tragic endings in Greek mythology?"

He laughs. "Pretty much. But some would say my writing is a tragedy in and of itself, so I'm already doing my culture justice. What do you like to do, Issy?"

"Oh no. I am not an Issy."

"Sorry, I didn't take you for a Dora."

"I'm not. I'm an Isadora."

"No nicknames?"

"My name is Isadora. That's who I am. I hate nicknames."

"I'm sorry. I didn't know it was a big deal." He sounds sincere.

I sigh. "It's not. Well, it is. It's just—cultural, right? Your name is who you are, what defines you. Ancient Egyptians even believed names themselves had power. You take away someone's name, or change it, you're taking away a part of them. You *are* your name." I frown, thinking of all my stupid relatives who couldn't ever even bother to learn my name. My mom, who'd call me pet names all the time—she couldn't be bothered to see *me*, Isadora. I was just another baby, just another kid to snuggle and raise to worship her, then replace.

"That makes perfect sense," he says.

"It's lame and we both know it. But don't you dare even *think* about calling me Dora."

"Deal. Isadora it is, and nothing else forever."

I risk a glance at him and he's staring at me with his brilliant secret smile, and I quickly turn and fix my eyes determinedly on the horizon; the water is losing its glow. I lie back, willing the constellations to show.

Ry does the same next to me, putting his arms behind his head. He starts saying something but is interrupted by my shriek as the first stars come out. "Yay!"

"What?"

"I've missed them so much! If only Orion were out."

"Umm, what are we talking about here?"

"My stars!" I point up. Now that I've seen them, some of the things that had detached inside of me settle into place, where they're supposed to be. My heart is actually fluttering in my chest I'm so excited. The only thing I need for it to be perfect is Orion. I have to wait a few more months until he's visible at night again, though.

"Your stars? And Orion?"

"The night I was born, Orion was the most prominent in the sky, and it's always been my favorite constellation. I can't wait for this winter. Orion's like the one constant in my life, the one thing I could always find when I needed comfort." It spills out; I shouldn't tell him anything, but I'm so relieved I'm giddy.

He laughs again. "Well, that's weird."

I turn and stick my tongue out at him. "Sure, Epic Poetry Boy."

"No, no, I don't mean the stars. I mean, what you were saying about names and how important they are."

"What does that have to do with anything?"

"Well, Isadora-not-Issy-or-Dora, I'm Ry—as in Orion." His smile shines in the dark like a beacon. Like my stars.

Chaos take me.

W ho are you remembering today?" Mother asks, beaming at me as I kneel in front of the small stone altar in my room.

"I'm remembering Thoth." He's my favorite. I love it when he visits.

Mother nods her approval. "Thoth is the reason I was born. And he helped me when your brother Horus was poisoned by Set."

I know these stories, but this is part of the worship, part of the remembering. In my head and my heart I list the things that Thoth is god of, and then I remember the stories I've been taught about him. Finally, I repeat his name to myself, and then trace it onto the altar.

Of course, I always do Isis and Osiris first. I think Mother would like me to do Horus more often than I do, but he ignores me and I'd always rather remember Thoth. Once a month I do a quick one of the rest of them—Nephthys, Hathor, Anubis, Set, Ammit, Grandma Nut, Grandpa Mun, and of course Amun-Re. I always shiver when I have to remember everything Set has done, though.

"You started a bit late this morning," my mother says.

I whisper Thoth's name, tracing it without looking up at her. My stomach twists guiltily. I slept in five minutes past dawn. "I'm sorry."

"We must always have order in this house. Everything has a time and a purpose. If we maintain order . . ."

"We never leave chaos an opening to creep in," I finish, and look up at her.

But she's gone. I look toward the door, but beyond it the hall is dark. Darker than dark, swirling and alive with blackness. The darkness has my mother.

I crawl backward, away from it, crunching across shards of broken glass I know shouldn't be there. I freeze. If I move, if I make a noise, the darkness will come for me, too.

Isis knew that, with Osiris already in the underworld, she needed another claim to the god-king throne of Egypt. She presented Horus to the other gods, magically conceived after Osiris's death, young but strong and ready to take his father's place. And at his side, his mother, who was willing to do anything to support him.

Nephthys wanted a son, too. But Set would not oblige her. So, dressed and made up to look like Isis, she approached a drunken Osiris. Anubis was born. And Nephthys slunk back into the shadows, begging her sister to shield them from Osiris's wrath and take Anubis as Isis's own son.

That's how Anubis is both my half brother and my cousin. Soap operas got nothing on my family history.

I WAVE AT SIRUS, AND THEN WAVE AGAIN, and then stop and put my hands on my hips until he slowly drives through the roundabout and away. He's been over-protective lately, of both Deena and me, and while I appreciate the sentiment, I hardly think he needs to worry about me at work. I even caught him yesterday, hanging out nearby. He claimed it was because he had nothing else to do and the day was beautiful, but finally admitted it was because Deena kicked him out of her office because he was making her feel claustrophobic.

I'm tired and my head aches and it's a relief that today, at least, I have something to do here. First the break-in, and now the ridiculous coincidence about Orion's—*Ry's*—name. My brain has been set on overdrive, and I can't get it to calm down. The fact that all of my mother's junk for the new exhibit finally showed up actually makes me excited. A day spent supervising the unpacking of a bunch of cracking, chipped depictions of my mother replacing my father's missing manhood with one made of clay, or nursing miniature pharaohs, or poisoning the sun god?

It's oddly comforting.

My phone buzzes in my pocket as I hurry out from under the enclosed walkway to the front of the museum . . . which is surrounded by police cars with their lights on. Four of them are pulled up on the sidewalk surrounding the stairs.

Floods, what is going on? I slide through a small gap between two of the cars and take the stairs three at a time in my stilettos. As soon as I go through the blue door, a police officer walks up to me, blocking my way.

"It's okay," Michelle says, sounding like it's anything but. She's flanked by two other officers, both of whom are writing on pads. "Isadora works here."

"What's wrong?" I ask, eyeing the congregation of uniformed men suspiciously. Why would they be here, too?

"There was a robbery attempt last night," Michelle says.

If I had known San Diego was so crime-ridden, maybe I would have opted to stay with my geriatric sister Essa, who works for a library in Cairo. "What did they take?" I ask.

"They didn't get anything, but a driver was seriously injured."

"Wait, driver? The delivery was attacked?"

She nods. "Right when the truck with your mother's artifacts got here. One of the security guards was opening the back door when the driver was jumped. Fortunately we had more security on duty. They came out and the robber ran off."

"That's good. I mean, bad." I shake my head. "My brother's house was broken into just last week." I pause, rubbing my arms against the chill that's settled there. "Wait, you don't think they're connected, do you?"

One of the officers next to her, a kind-looking man with a shaved head, frowns. "Did you have anything related to the exhibit? Anything that tied you to the artifacts?"

"No." Well, besides Sirus and me, who are genetically tied to them. And my amulets that were smashed up. But obviously no one thought they were valuable or worth stealing. "They didn't take anything. The police figure it was some guy looking for prescription drugs."

"Probably no connection then. Still, keep a close eye out from now on, and if you see anything weird—here or at home—let us know immediately." He hands me his card, then leaves as another officer waves him over.

I put the card in my wallet, then look back at Michelle. "How did the robber know the truck was getting here?" *We* didn't even know it would be here today. Michelle called last night after she found out what time it would arrive to make sure I was ready.

"That's what we're trying to figure out. The current theory is that whoever it was didn't know—they must have been watching for it."

"Who would want to steal a bunch of old crap?"

Michelle raises her eyebrows. "Isadora, you do know this exhibit is priceless, right?"

I resist the urge to roll my eyes. You can't throw a rock in my house without hitting some "priceless" artifact. "Is the driver okay?"

She looks away, like she doesn't want to answer me. "He's in the hospital."

I swallow against my suddenly dry throat. "Will he *be* okay?"

"They aren't sure yet. Most of his major organs are failing."

"He was shot?"

"No. They think poison, but they have no idea what."

A shiver trails down my spine. That doesn't sound good. None of this sounds good. I hate that the museum now feels as exposed and vulnerable as Sirus's house, and

I can't help but think the only connection—even though it makes no sense—is me. But why would any robber think we'd store that kind of stuff in our house?

Michelle shakes her head like she's trying to brush off the same chills plaguing my arms. "Anyway, we're closed today, probably tomorrow, too."

"Is there anything I can do?"

"When we reopen, I'll recruit you to help decorate the big hallway we're converting into a new wing for the exhibit. Your mother said you're good with design."

A strange, warm feeling floods through me. It feels suspiciously like pride. My mother said that?

"What in the holy heck is going on?" Tyler yells from where she is being blocked entry by one of the police officers.

Waving wearily, Michelle says, "Fill her in. I'll send out an email with more details and when we'll reopen." I nod, then walk to Tyler in the entrance. She lets me take her by the elbow and escort her back outside. We sit down across the street, watching the lights from the cop cars.

"Well, I didn't see that coming," she says as I finish telling her everything. "But it's really your mom's stuff? As in, it *belongs* to her? Can people even own ancient Egyptian artifacts?"

I shrug, not sure how to answer. "I guess they can."

"You guys must be, like, obscenely rich. Did you travel everywhere when you were growing up?"

106

"We'd go to Cairo every once in a while, and visit some of the cities around us, but it was mainly day trips to the Nile."

"Fancy cars?"

"Don't have one."

"Please tell me you at least have a private jet."

"I don't think my parents have ever even been on a plane. The flights here were my very first time."

"Oh, for the love. Some people should not be allowed to be rich."

I shrug. "And apparently some people will kill to get rich." I look back at the doors. Today the building looming over us feels vaguely sinister. Who else has been watching it, waiting? Are they still out there? Are they watching me, too?

"Yeah, that sucks for the driver. Well, I promise to think about him on our days off." She pulls out her phone and texts furiously while I lean back and let the sun play on my face. The clouds are spotty today—it feels miraculous that there isn't a total cover. I miss dry heat. I miss the way you can feel the air when you breathe it in, like the landscape is making you part of itself, entering you with every breath.

Sirus told me that in the fall they get Santa Ana winds like the desert. It's his favorite time of the year; I can't wait.

I look at Tyler. "You want to come to my brother's house? He has a . . . television. And a swimming pool."

Tyler stands, offering me her hand. "Yes. I absolutely want to. But today Scott's over at Ry's house. Something about video games. My car's over here."

She starts walking, and I hesitate on the steps. "You know, I think . . . I'm just gonna go home." I feel shaky and nervous, and the thought of being around Ry doesn't promise an improvement on that.

"Why? We have a day off!"

"I remembered I'm supposed to help my sister-in-law with some remodeling stuff." She wants me to do the nursery. Working in pastels makes me want to strangle myself with pale-pink curtains, but she said she had something else in mind. We were actually going to plan it tonight since she's at work all day. However, Tyler doesn't need to know that.

"Yeah, but she can't be counting on your help today because you had work! So you're not missing anything you're expected to be there for."

I curse inwardly. She wasn't supposed to figure that out. I can't admit it's because I don't want to see Ry. It's too weird. And it's even weirder that I can't stop thinking that it's weird. It shouldn't matter what his name is. It shouldn't.

It still does.

"Can you just give me a ride home, please?"

She sighs. "Sure. But I am not happy."

Tyler drives away after making me swear to call if I finish early. I feel genuinely bad about lying to her, so I slip out of my heels and walk upstairs to the spare room. If I actually work on it, it wasn't lying.

The room is completely blank, not even curtains on the window. Ideas for a retro polka-dot theme spin through my mind. Large circles on the walls, painted in contrasting colors. Circles cut out of Styrofoam and plastered to the ceiling, painted the same color but for a textural accent. Round-back rocking chair with a circular ottoman.

There's nothing but potential here, and I can't wait to get started. As much as I loathe the idea of wasting all of the work on a baby, I can have fun with this. And it will prove to Sirus and Deena that I should do the rest of the house, too.

I pull out my phone and call Deena. "Hey, I'm home early and wanted to start on the room. You said you had an inspiration folder?"

"Yes! It's in the box marked 'tampons and bathroom stuff.' I didn't want Sirus to see it."

I laugh, cradling the phone against my shoulder. All of the boxes have been opened, and the one she told me about is empty. "Are you sure? There's nothing here. What am I looking for?"

"It's just a black binder, one of Sirus's childhood scrapbooks. It has a lot of pictures of murals and ancient Egyptian art. I wanted to do a theme nursery."

Oh, floods. She wants me to create the room I spent my whole childhood working on.

No. This isn't a tomb, and it's not mine. I can do it for her.

I pick up the box again, shake it. "I don't see it anywhere. All of the boxes are open. Are you sure Sirus didn't move it?"

"No, he's not allowed in that room, he wouldn't have. No one has been in there."

Then it hits me—the memory creeping down my arms in a physical sensation like I'm being watched. This bedroom door was open. It was open, the day of the break-in. I'd never seen it open before. Deena *always* keeps it closed. "This room is the first room in the hall," I say, my voice soft. "Maybe it was the intruder."

"Why would someone take it?" she asks, bewildered and hurt.

I have no answers.

I wake up with a gasping start from the nap I'd only just fallen into. Every noise the house makes sounds suspect. Hopefully the thing with the folder really is just a misunderstanding and we'll find it in some weird place later, but I feel like eyes are watching me. And I can't quit thinking about that driver being attacked and poisoned. Somehow that scares me far more than him being shot would have. Shooting is impersonal; it only happens in movies.

Poison is something my family understands intimately.

The dark corners of the house seem alive, menacing,

110

and I can feel myself starting to lose it. I don't want to be alone. I want to be with someone who always makes me feel lighter. I walk out to the porch and pull out my phone.

"I knew you'd call," Tyler says without saying hello.

"I didn't get my daily dose of Tyler at the museum today."

"Tyler deficiencies can be fatal, you know. I'll come get you right now."

"Thanks." I'm so grateful I don't even know how to express it. However, when it's not Tyler's small Toyota that pulls up but rather Ry's beautiful truck, I'm torn between that gratitude and annoyance.

"Hey," he says, climbing out of the truck and walking up the short, cracked sidewalk to where I'm sitting on the porch. "Tyler told me to come pick you up."

"Of course she did." I ignore his extended hand and push myself to standing. Ry manages to be a couple inches taller than me even in my heels. Huh. I'd hoped I would be taller than him. I really like being taller than people.

I follow him to the truck. "Did you hurt your leg?" I ask. He has a slight limp I'd never noticed. Not that I was noticing things about him now, like the way his dark hair somehow reflected gold bits in the sun, or how his shoulders created a straight, strong line across his back. Or the pronounced bump of a callus on his middle right finger.

"No, I've always had a limp. It runs in my family."

So he isn't perfect. Physically, I mean. I don't mean that. He's not perfect at all.

I hate Tyler.

Ry tries to beat me to my side, but I manage to slide in before he can open the door. He gets in, and the truck engine turns over much too quietly. I wish it'd roar. I wish it'd growl so loud I wouldn't be able to hear my own thoughts. I hate that I'm scared in a place I should feel safe. I hate that it's spread to my work. I hate that I'm so self-centered that I think it somehow revolves around me.

I want to call my mom.

I won't.

Ry drives confidently, eyes on the road, and I watch him shift gears to see how it's done. I should probably learn how to drive. "You never did tell me what you like to do for fun," he says.

"Interior design." If he laughs, I will disembowel him. And I won't even put his guts into ceremonial jars for embalmment—I'll scatter them across the dirt. I'll toss them into the garbage disposal.

"So you're an artist."

Oh. Well, that was unexpected. "I guess."

"That's really cool. I'd love to see your designs some-time."

I'm caught off guard again. I don't know how to respond, so I change the subject. "Where are we going?"

"My house. Tyler and Scott are there already."

I try to tamp down my intrigue. People's homes say so much about them, and even though it will really only say stuff about Ry's parents, I'm still interested.

"How do you and Tyler and Scott know each other? Do you all go to the same school?"

"I actually met Tyler at Balboa Park last summer. We don't go to the same school. But I like them. Neither of them cares that I have a tendency toward being antisocial, and Tyler never tries to flirt with me. Scott doesn't, either."

I roll my eyes. "So that's your main requirement for friendship? They don't hit on you? Is that like a regular problem in your life?"

He shrugs noncommittally. "Isn't it in yours?"

I frown, thinking of all of the guys I interact with. I do get hit on a lot at the museum. I just don't care because I'd as soon be left alone.

When I don't answer, he smiles. "It's hard to be friends with girls most of the time."

Oh, shut up. He is *not* saying that he's too good-looking to be friends with girls. But then again, at the beach there *were* a high percentage of beauties sitting very close to us and/or sauntering repeatedly past. And he never looked up once. I snort. "You poor handsome thing. If only you were ugly, then girls wouldn't have to throw themselves at you all the time. I could break your perfect nose for you, if it'd make your life easier."

He raises his eyebrows as if he's considering it, then

shakes his head. "I think my mom would be upset," he says finally, a genuine note of regret in his voice.

"Maybe next time, then." What if he had really asked me to? I laugh. I can see it, me trying and failing to break his nose. I'm not actually a violent person, in spite of being raised on bedtime stories of war and conquest and murder. I was also raised on stories of sex, and I'm not interested in that, either.

We leave the main road and wind through neighborhoods that are familiar, though I don't remember why. I can see glints of the ocean from here, and then we pull up into a driveway.

A driveway I already know.

Oh, floods. My mockery echoes perfectly in my ears. Of course. Of course it's his house we parked at when we went to the beach.

"Yours?" I ask, my voice coming out as a pathetic squeak.

He nods, a smile pulling apart his full lips. I fight back the shame burning in my face. Yes, my comments were rude. But Ry could have told me it was his house, instead of letting me look like a jerk.

We get out of the truck and climb the broad steps. Ry pushes one of the massive, carved white double doors open. It's like we've stepped into a museum of Greek antiquities. The floor is polished marble, with black tiles scrolling a pattern around the borders of the entry.

A bust of a woman, the pure definition of beautiful, is on a pedestal front and center, and various other sculptures line the room. Almost laughably out of place is a single humongous framed photo of a chubby, cherubic little boy, face smeared with cake as he laughs at the camera.

"My parents take our heritage very seriously," he says, his voice solemn but his eyes twinkling as he looks at me to judge my reaction.

"Really? I dunno, it's kind of understated."

He laughs appreciatively, and I'm relieved that at least he has a sense of humor about the whole thing.

"The tile work is amazing," I say, wanting to make up for my earlier mockery, and because it's true. This floor is gorgeous.

Tyler pokes her head out of a side hall. "There you are! You okay, Isadora? Your call seemed panicked."

I wave my hand dismissively. "I'm fine." There are no bogeymen. I need to get over this.

"Good! I'm glad you came. Come on," she says. We follow her through a hallway with dark wood paneling and the same marble floor, but covered in a plush, ornate rug.

I approve of the TV room we go into as Tyler runs off to use the bathroom. Someone seems to have abandoned the formality of the rest of the house—framed movie posters dominate the walls, and the biggest television I've ever seen in my life takes up the entirety of one wall. A full bar lines the back of the room.

I wouldn't change a lot. The movie-poster thing is really cute. I'd use shadow-box frames and backlighting though. Switch out the L-shaped sectional for one long couch and a few movie-theater-style armchairs. Heavy drapes to block out the light better—the white shutter blinds are totally out of place. Redo the beige walls a pale gold, keep the baseboards their rich cherry color, and, ooh, put in maroon velvet drapes covering not just the wide window but the entire wall. Taking the fun atmosphere of the room up a notch or two. Also, a popcorn machine on top of the bar so the whole place smells right.

But no one's asking me.

A hugely fat white Persian cat skulks into the room. Still planning my changes, I reach down and scratch her ears absently as she twines her way around my legs, purring like a street bike.

"Whoa."

"Whoa what?" I ask. Ry is staring in amazement at the cat.

"Hera doesn't like *anyone*."

"Oh." I look down. Her sharp, intelligent eyes regard me with something bordering on playful worship, like we're in on the same eternal joke. There's a reason cats were near deity in ancient Egypt. Dogs may be loyal, but cats are smart. This one must recognize our bond. You can take the cat out of Egypt, but you can't take Egypt out of the cat.

Wow, I should have that embroidered on a pillow or something.

With a pang I'm reminded of Ubesti. I never let my parents get me another pet after her. Just another thing to love and lose. I gently shoo Ry's cat away with my foot. She mews reproachfully and saunters out of the room.

Ry watches her go, eyes narrowed, then shakes his head. "Want anything?" he asks Scott, who's engrossed in a video game. It's so big on the television that I don't know how he can keep track of anything going on.

"Nah, I'm good."

"Coke, Isadora?"

"Yes, please."

He pulls a cold can out of a hidden fridge in the bar and hands it to me. "So."

"So?"

"The entryway is off-limits, but what would you do with this room?"

"What makes you think I'd do anything with it?"

His dimple shows up. "You glared at the blinds."

"It's a great room! Really. But . . ." My mouth twists into a reluctant smile. I detail my plans, and Ry nods, following my finger as I point out what would go and what could stay.

". . . And the overhead lighting is pretty, but wrong for

this room. There shouldn't be any fixtures, just recessed lights along the edges of the room, with a dimmer so you could control the level."

"I should have you talk to my mom," he says, thoughtfully staring at where the popcorn machine would go.

"Is she here?" Scott sits up straight, suddenly engaged in the conversation.

"Don't think so."

"Aw, crap."

"Plans for hitting on DeeDee thwarted?" Tyler asks as she walks into the room and sits next to Scott.

"Sadly, yes."

"Wait—you want to—his mom?" Eww. Just, eww. People suck. "You're okay with that, Tyler?"

Tyler shrugs, her sharp shoulders lifting the corners of her mouth at the same time. "Yeah. But only because I'd probably make out with her if I got the chance, too. You should see her."

I look at Ry in horror, embarrassed for his sake, but he shakes his head. "Used to it."

"Really, you need to see her," Tyler insists.

"Really, I can promise you that I'll have no desire whatsoever to hit on Ry's mom if and when I see her. Ever."

Tyler and Scott snort their private laughter. "Sure. If you think Ry's gorgeous, just wait."

"Who says I think Ry's gorgeous?" I say, raising an eyebrow.

"Nature pretty much demands it. Unless—are you a robot?" Scott slaps his forehead. "Of course!"

Tyler nods solemnly. "We should have seen it sooner. That long, elegant neck, those eyes, the hips, the perpetual good-hair days. Totally a robot."

"The only question that remains is whether she's a good robot, or an evil one."

"Well, Hera liking you might indicate you're evil," Ry says. "But then again, nothing evil could appreciate my truck as much as you do. Speaking of, can I offer you rides anywhere you want for the rest of the summer in return for redesigning my bedroom?"

"Time for us to go!" Tyler says, standing up so fast she dumps Scott, who had his legs across her lap, on the ground. "Just remembered we have a thing! I'll call you later!" She practically skips out of the room, dragging her grinning boyfriend by the hand.

That blonde? Evil. I'm going to make her take every Children's Discovery Room shift for a month.

"So," Ry says, turning toward me, his face a picture of innocence but his eyes doing that thing where they erase the rest of the world. "You think they want us to get together?"

I choke on my mouthful of Coke, narrowly avoiding spewing it all down my front, then focus on Ry, glaring. If he thinks I'm going to be coy about this, he's wrong. I refuse to flirt. "Yeah, actually, I do think she's trying to set us up."

He nods. "Tyler tends to go into mother-hen mode. She thinks I'm by myself too often, and obviously thinks the same of you, which in her mind turns into making us a couple."

"I'm not going to date you."

He has the nerve to look puzzled, and—oh floods, are you kidding me—sad. "Have I done something to you?"

"I—no. It's not you. I'm not going to date anyone. Ever."

"Really?" He sits down on the couch like he expects me to follow suit. I stay standing.

"Really. I have no desire whatsoever to date and get married and have kids."

"The one doesn't lead immediately to the others, you know. There are stages in between, or so I've heard. Could be a rumor, though."

I roll my eyes. "Whatever. What's the point? Nothing lasts forever. Relationships only hurt."

Sometimes I wonder if my parents ever loved each other. They barely exist on the same plane. My dad cheated on my mom with her sister, whether or not he meant to, and she still pulled out all the stops to resurrect him. For what? A husband who'd rather be in the underworld than in ours.

And in spite of all that, they have each other, forever. They last forever, their marriage lasts forever, there is no loss, no breaking up, no inevitability of death. I think if

I fell in love with someone, I'd never be able to breathe, never be able to function because of the fear.

I'm already going to lose myself. I never want to have to deal with losing someone else, too.

"That's kind of bleak," Ry says. "I think you're wrong."

"What do you know about it?" I snap.

Ry shrugs. "My parents broke up."

"Oh. I'm sorry." Deflated, I sit gingerly on the edge of the couch. Great, Isadora. Brilliant. Make fun of his house and then bring up his own family pain. Sometimes I forget I'm not the only one with a past. Ry's a real person, too.

"Nah, it's okay. It was a long time ago. My mom thought she wanted other things, and my dad couldn't forgive her for it. They spent a while chasing different lives and being unhappy, and then they got back together. They've been pretty good ever since."

"That must have been really hard for you."

"I wasn't born yet. But none of us is perfect, right? And if you love someone, you have to deal with that. If you ask me, love is what makes everything worth it. Otherwise what's the point of anything? Besides, I'm glad they worked it out. I kinda like existing." He nudges me with his elbow, grinning, and I have to smile back.

"Fine. But I say, skip loving someone so you never *have* to deal with it."

He doesn't look away from my eyes, trapping me in

the perfect blue of his, then claps his hands together like he's come to a decision. "Are you also morally opposed to being friends? Does that mysteriously lead to immediate babies, too?"

My heart flutters a tiny bit—like it knows maybe I'm in trouble here, like it'd rather steel up and have me flip him off, or laugh in his face, or shrug him away. But he's a real person to me now, someone with pain and weirdness and heartache woven into the narrative of his life. And he seems sincere, and it might be nice to have a friend in addition to Tyler.

"I guess not," I finally answer, well aware that I paused far too long before responding. But friendship isn't something that should be taken lightly, right? "Although Tyler will be way happier about it than she deserves to be."

"I think she deserves to be happy. And now that we're friends, can I get your advice on my room? It's pretty bad."

"How bad are we talking?"

"Two words: sports theme."

"Floods, we'd better get started. What did you have in mind?"

He looks at me for a long time before smiling. "I'm thinking a color scheme of browns with accents of hunter green." He holds out a hand to help me up from the couch, and as I take it and feel his hand around mine in a shock of human contact and something more, that part that warned me of trouble is proved absolutely right.

*S*obs rack my body as I slam my door shut behind me.

They don't want me.

They don't want me.

It's a tomb! I'm going to die! They've known it this whole time!

Exhausted from rage and grief, I do what I always do when I need to calm down, and kneel in front of the altar in my room.

"No," I say, filled with horror. Because as I stare at the altar, I realize that no one prays to me. No one prays to my brother Sirus, or my sister Essa, or any of us. Because we don't matter.

I fall back, feeling like the altar has punched a hole in my chest. Of course they don't need me to last forever. My mother has a baby every twenty years. A new one to train up in the ways of worshipping herself and her family.

We're not children. We're power sources.

Screaming, I stand and kick the altar. It doesn't move. I brace myself against the wall and kick against it as hard as I can, and it slowly leans until gravity takes over and it crashes to the ground, breaking into three pieces.

I sniffle, wipe my eyes. An inky darkness, like oil and fog, seeps out of the broken pieces, getting bigger, wider, darker. It oozes toward the door, toward where my mother waits on the other side, asking if she can come in.

"Mom?" I whisper, all my anger frozen into fear.

She doesn't answer.

||||
||||

"Take my son," begged Nephthys, voice a whisper, eyes down. "Shield him from the wrath of Osiris."

Isis looked at the boy, the son of her husband and her sister. She looked at her sister. She held out her arms.

Anubis was the son of Osiris. Isis protected him the way Nephthys couldn't, then sent him to the underworld to take a place by his father's side. She found him an inheritance, a role, a domain to be a god in.

But she wanted more for Horus. Horus would have the crown of all Egypt.

Maybe she used up all of her maternal energy on him, because the rest of us just got dead cats in jars.

"THIS IS THE MOST STRAIGHTFORWARDLY named restaurant I have ever seen." I stare up at the sign declaring we are about to eat at Extraordinary Desserts. There's a funky, bright brushed-metal latticework glamming up the outside of the one-story building, and I already love the look of the place. It's day two of my Official Friendship with Ry. I think these things should always be declared officially. It makes it much less complicated when he invites me to go get food. Friends do that, and I know we're friends. No reason to overthink.

"It's not false advertising," Ry says. We walk in through a huge black door and are greeted by display cases of the desserts, which, floods, look extraordinary.

I lean over the glass. Even the names of the desserts taste like sugar in my mouth. Flower petals adorn the most beautiful plates of food I've ever seen. Some even have gold-flake accents. I will spend my entire daily allowance here. "I want everything."

"Bread pudding," Ry says.

I raise an eyebrow, dubious. "Bread pudding. We're staring at rows of cheesecake and chocolate and fruit tarts and cake, and you want to eat bread . . . mixed with pudding."

Ry nods. "Trust me. We'll get a few other things, but once you've had the bread pudding, you won't ever want anything else here."

I don't trust him on that at all. We sit down outside and order. I get a pot of tea, the afternoon chill from the clouds barely enough to justify it.

"How do you feel about Indian food?" Ry asks, toying with his napkin. He's wearing a heather-gray tee today, and I like it but I prefer him in blue.

I mean, I have no preferences. I don't care what he wears. Just the aesthetics, that's all. "I'm game for anything. I grew up on about five different meals rotated on an eternal basis, so this is all good."

"You're lucky we're friends." His dimple is the exclamation mark to his cocky grin.

I shake my head, but I smile, too. "I could find restaurants by myself. I do know how to use the internet."

"Ah, but you never would have ordered bread pudding. You need me."

I drum my fingers on the table, then snap. "I almost forgot! Here." I pull out my black messenger bag. "I needed to pick up a new notebook with graph paper, and I noticed your notebook was almost full, so I . . ." I trail off, holding out a deep-blue, leather-bound notebook. Well, journal, really. Nicer than the one I'd seen him using, but this was so beautiful and when I saw the color I thought instantly of Ry.

"Seriously?" His face lights up, so honestly delighted that I want to laugh. Something flutters in my stomach, and I hope it simply means I'm hungry.

"I'm enabling your antisocial tendencies." In part it's an I'm-sorry gift, though I'd never say so out loud. I realized yesterday that he didn't laugh at me when I said my passion was interior design, but I had been kind of a jerk about his writing. I actually like it about him, like that he has such a bizarre focus and pastime.

He takes the book, flipping through the pages, fingering them gently. "I'm not feeling very antisocial today," he says.

Neither am I. The waitress comes, and I drown my

flutters in herbal tea. And then bread pudding, which is warm and soft, with just the right balance of rich dark chocolate and cool, sweet cream.

Ry laughs, because he doesn't even have to ask me if I like it. I've already eaten the whole thing and am plotting the soonest moment I can come back for another.

"So," Tyler says, leaning in conspiratorially while Michelle finishes a phone call next to us. "You and Ry have been spending a lot of time together the last couple days."

"Mmm," I answer.

"How's that going?" She waggles her eyebrows in undisguised glee.

"I am more likely to end up romantically involved with his cat than him."

The glee falls off her face. "You—what? Gosh, if I'd known you had a thing for long-haired Persians, I'd have set you up with my family's landlord."

I snort and shove her shoulder. "Seriously. Ry and I are friends. That's it."

"Ooookay. Sure. If you say so. Speaking of friends, what are you doing this weekend? I'm thinking a movie marathon. As long as snuggling up on a couch in a dim room next to Ry for hours on end won't interfere with this whole *friends* thing you're rocking . . ."

"Not an issue. But maybe invite your landlord, too, since he's clearly more my type."

Tyler jumps in surprise as Michelle lets out an explosive swearing tirade next to me. That much foulness coming out of her tiny body never ceases to amuse me, especially because it so rarely happens.

"The insurers won't let us set up the pieces until the night before the exhibit opens. They want everything to stay in the high-security storage center until the last possible moment. How are we supposed to get everything ready when we can't even place the artifacts?"

Huffing, she stomps up the stairs toward the wing we're going to be using. I haven't seen it yet.

Really, though, I can't blame them for being paranoid about security. The poor guard is still in intensive care in the hospital; he's on several organ-donor lists. They have no idea what happened to him, which makes it all way creepier. And I'm grateful that Michelle was too nervous to give my mother specifics on the attempted robbery, otherwise I'm pretty sure I'd be on the next flight back to Cairo. It had nothing to do with me, anyway.

Besides, it's hard to feel threatened here in the daytime, the cheerful, bright warmth pushing out the memory of June gloom and everything else dark or dreary.

The nights are another matter. But sunshine! I will focus on that.

The sunshine I'm focusing on barely makes it into the room Michelle opens. Even I am at a loss as to how they thought this would ever work. It's not really a room so much as a massive hallway, stretching two-thirds the entire length of the building. It's got tremendously high ceilings, 3.7 meters I'd guess, but it's only about 2.5 meters wide.

Half of a wall has the remnants of some ill-begotten mural celebrating Central American indigenous cultures, and the rest of the walls are all splotchy white. A tiny row of windows lined up near the ceiling on the right side lets in a dusty trickle of natural light.

Her rage gone as if it never existed, Michelle studies the room as though her efficient, business-oriented gaze could whip it into shape by sheer force of will. "I still think we should disassemble one of the other exhibits and store it in here. Use a main room."

"I am not disassembling that gigantic tree of evolution," Tyler says, setting down a broom and leaning against the wall.

Michelle nods. "You're probably right. We should have all the other exhibits open to avoid bottlenecking this one." She gestures to a wall. "We can continue the color scheme from the Egypt wing—greens and purples and maybe a mural, then—"

"For the love of these idiot gods, anything but that."

Michelle and Tyler both look at me, shocked. I shrug apologetically. "Didn't mean to say that out loud. No offense, but the Egypt room needs an update. Let's think of something new."

Raising an eyebrow, Michelle smiles. "So, what should we do?"

I look down the length of the room and then close my eyes. An image of my father's hall pops unbidden into my mind: the carved stone, the patterns, the murals, Ammit in her eternal watch, his low throne at the end. The weight of age and the gravity of death.

No.

The Nile, then? A green-blue floor, the walls yellow and lined with rushes. A breeze, the ripe-but-comforting scent of things wet too long. Still not quite right. Not enough sun in the room. Maybe if we could install heat lamps to leave the air dry and baking, but somehow I doubt that'll fly.

Behind the darkness of my eyelids, lights trace lazy patterns as always, and I'm reminded of my stars. I cringe back from the idea because it would bring too much of my home here. But no. I'm over that. I will reclaim that idea. I'm going to remake my past so it can't hurt me anymore. Just like the nursery I'll do for Deena. I can remove the pain from these things instead of carrying it with me forever.

"Got it!" I open my eyes, the plans for the room spinning out in front of my vision, already replacing this sad space. "Stars."

"Stars?" Tyler stands up straight, frowning.

"Stars. So much of ancient Egypt was focused on life

outside of this one—our dreams, our souls, our deaths, the afterlife. They knew more about astronomy than any other culture at the time, always looking forward and backward and outward. So we paint the room pure black, and—no, we don't even have to do that."

I wander up and down, looking for outlets, studying the ceiling. "Here's what we'll need: huge sheets of plywood. It'll bring the walls in a few inches on either side, but we can afford to lose the space. And lowering the ceiling a bit will help with the effect. The windows need to be blocked entirely. We paint the plywood all black and drill holes for LED lights. I can map out the star charts. My mother's pieces will be staggered throughout, along the walls and in the middle, lit from beneath and by their own pedestals, so that they stand out in the middle of eternity."

Michelle looks at the room with narrowed eyes. "It sounds complicated. And expensive."

"It'll only be the cost of materials, and we can do them cheap."

"What about the time? We don't have much. I'll have to get it approved before you can start, and it might take a week or two for clearance."

"I can do it. I know I can do it." I bite my lip, hoping she'll agree. Now that I've decided what the room should be, doing anything else will be a disappointment.

Finally, she nods. "Okay. Prove what you can do. And if you do a good job, I might be able to let you redecorate some of our older exhibits that you seem to think need updates."

"Thank you!" I say, already racing with adrenaline and ready to work. I will own this room. I will own my past. I will own my future.

"Isadora!"

"Mother!" I sit straight up in bed, heart racing. This isn't the tomb, or my bed, or my home.

Deena stands in my doorway, hand on her nearly non-existent hip. I swear, that baby is taking over her entire small frame. How she doesn't split open down the middle is a mystery to me. "Your friend's here."

"My friend?" I run my fingers through my hair, which is sticking out at crazy angles all over my head. "Tyler?"

"The boy?" She leans into the room conspiratorially. "The incredibly, ridiculously hot boy?"

I slap my forehead and flop back down. "What time is it?"

"Eleven."

"Floods, who gets up before noon on a day when they don't have anything going on?" I couldn't sleep in the first few days, my well-trained internal alarm jolting me awake immediately. So I've started staying up as late as physically possible to force my body into needing the extra sleep in the morning. Who knew being lazy was such hard work?

"He's already in the room priming. He's been here for

over an hour, told me not to wake you. I figured it had been long enough."

With a growl I throw back the covers and stomp down the hall to the nursery.

Ry's in a light-blue T-shirt and worn-out jeans. Three-quarters of the room is already primed, and music plays softly from an iPod dock in the corner. When I demanded that Ry pay me back for advising him on his travesty of a bedroom, I hadn't expected him to take me up on it willingly—or quickly.

"What's wrong with you?" I ask, squinting against the brilliant light streaming in through the blank, undressed window.

"Hmm?" He looks over, and his face breaks into a smile—chaos, how does he do that? It's like his whole body glows. It scatters my waking grouchiness, and I can feel a glow warming me, too. "Wasn't I supposed to help?"

"Well, yeah, but I thought I'd have to drag you over here or something."

He shrugs and goes back to the wall. "Nah, it's kind of fun. Sorry for just showing up, but I didn't have anything else to do this morning."

"No writing? Your muse isn't speaking to you?"

"She rarely does. International call charges and whatnot. Besides which, she's flighty and nearly impossible to understand. And she says I always misinterpret her intentions."

"Muses. What can you do, right?" I run my fingers through my hair again, back and forth, making it stand up even more. I could use a shower. Then again, if I'm going to paint, might as well wait. And it's not like I care what Ry thinks of my hair. Or my smell.

I stretch and surreptitiously sniff myself in case. Not that you can smell anything over the itchy chemical scent of the paint, but there's no reason to stink in front of anyone if you don't have to. I can let my eye makeup go this once, but I refuse to smell bad, ever.

"All right then," I say with a sigh, "let's do this thing."

The canvas is rough and bunched up under my feet, and I run back to my room to change into a grubbier set of pajamas. I've mostly got everything back in order from the break-in, but some of the drawers were damaged and won't open anymore, so I've been using my suitcase as extra storage. Reaching into the corner of one of the gaping pockets, I frown. Burlap? I pull out the tiny package and stare dumbly at it until it sinks in.

Ingredients. Pendants. My mom packed me an emergency magic kit, and these pendants aren't broken. For some reason it makes me feel happy, safer. Which kind of annoys me.

Skipping back to the nursery, I grab a roller and start at the opposite end of the last wall. I'm glad Ry's a fast worker—I hate priming rooms. It leaves your whole body sore and accomplishes nothing except setting the stage for more work. Ry doesn't talk, humming softly along to the music as he carefully and methodically paints.

"What is this?" I ask. We both keep our eyes on our rollers, moving slowly but surely toward each other.

"Hmm?"

"This song. 'Oh, hey, it's okay that I slept with you and left the next morning without a word, because someday someone will love you.' Seriously?"

He laughs. "I dunno, it has a nice message: we'll all find love eventually."

"That's not the message at all! That's the excuse! He's saying it's okay he used her because someday someone will actually love her, unlike him. Dude deserves to be castrated, if you ask me."

Ry chokes a bit, a strangled laugh. "Remind me never to piss you off."

"Whatever. See what I mean though? He's using her; she's crying and waiting for the day when someone won't. What kind of a life would that be? Screw it. I can be whole without depending on someone else, thank you very much."

"You can't really love someone romantically unless you're already whole anyway, though. So you're right on that count."

"But if you're whole, you don't *need* to love anyone."

"But how can you really be whole if you can't allow that part of yourself its portion of your life?"

"Romance is not a requirement for a happy life."

"I strongly and completely disagree. But however you feel about romance, love is definitely a requirement. Like your family. You can't be whole without them, right?"

They can be whole without *me*. All they do is pop out another baby, another battery to brainwash into worshipping them. I jam my roller furiously against the wall, too much paint oozing out of the pores of the roller and splotching my even stroke. "Families *make* holes. They don't fill them."

Brilliant. Now I have to go back over that section to even out the paint. Before I'm finished, Ry's made his way over and is standing right next to me.

"I'm sorry." His voice is soft and he stands there, waiting, until I finally look up into his face. "Do you want to talk about it?" I feel his eyes swallowing me, all kindness and understanding. I know I could tell him. Part of me wants to tell him, more than anything I've ever wanted, to spill out all the pain and betrayal and years of heartache, let it drop out of me and onto him and finally relieve all this pressure that I carry around until I feel like I'm going to burst from the strain of *hurting* so much and trying so hard not to care.

I drop my roller onto the canvas. "How about some of that magic Ry restauranting? I need food."

He smiles, smoothing out the rest of my splotched paint. "That I can do."

Set had worked too hard murdering Osiris to let a magically conceived heir take the throne he had rightfully stolen. While Set was older and stronger, with far more power on his side, Horus had something he didn't:

Isis.

Isis stole Horus away in the middle of the night, hiding him from danger, biding her time until he was old enough to inherit the throne. She enlisted the help of seven scorpions to protect her son. When a local village denied them sanctuary, the scorpions were enraged. Combining their poison, they stung the young son of one of the villagers.

He was near dying, his mother beside herself with grief, when Isis descended onto the scene, using the names of the scorpions to save the boy from the very gates of death. His mother was so overjoyed that she gave all she had to Isis.

Of course, no one dared point out that it was Isis's fault the scorpions were hanging around in the first place.

"OH, SHUT UP." I LAUGH AROUND A MOUTHFUL of gyro. Yesterday Ry took me to the "best" sushi around. I didn't care for the eel, but the California roll grew on me. I don't get seaweed, though. Texturally and taste-wise, it makes no sense.

Today's food, however, is effortless to enjoy.

"No, really," he says.

"You do not love that statue. It's an atrocity."

"I absolutely love it." Ry's face is straight but his eyes betray him, merry dancing sapphires. "It's tasteful, understated. Like the life-size bust of my mother in our entryway."

I snort, barely able to keep my last bite from spraying out. We're sitting on the grass at the harbor, surrounded by trees, in front of one of the strangest statues I've seen in my life. It's a sailor, tipping back a woman in a passionate kiss. But it's *huge*. Swallowing, I say, "I probably come up to the top of her shoe. From far away it looks kind of normal. Until you get close, then it's *bam, humongous giants making out on the grass*. In fact, I think that may be the title of the sculpture."

"If it's not, it should be." Ry leans back happily as we watch tourists take pictures beneath the behemoths.

"And why that pose? Her spine must be killing her after all these years of being tipped back."

"It comes from a really iconic photograph."

"Huh. Probably worked better as a picture."

"Yup. How's the gyro?"

"Meh, you know. So-so."

"Really?"

I shrug. "I've had better."

"And that's why you've inhaled it."

I lick the remnants of cucumber sauce off the waxed paper. "I don't like to waste food."

"Mmm-hmm." He watches me suspiciously, and I try to avoid giving away how amazing the gyro really was. He wasn't kidding—this is the best Greek food I've ever had. Which isn't saying too much, since my mom would never have consented to make it, but still.

"Okay, fine," I say. "I love it so much I might agree to skip past friends and dating and have its little gyro babies. But you can't take credit for this food, anyway."

"No?"

"Nope. The spicy meat? The cool cucumber sauce? Totally stole it. You Greeks and your culture theft."

"Is it theft if you take something and improve on it?"

"Let's add delusions of superiority to the list of things that are wrong with you."

"*Me* me, or Greeks in general?"

"*You* you. I'll try not to hold you against your people."

"Fair enough. Though you do know your name is Greek, right?"

I gasp. "It is not!"

"Is so. Look it up online. Isadora means Gift of the Moon."

"*No*, it means Gift of Isis, who was also goddess of the moon on occasion. And it's from when the Greeks went ahead and stole worship of Egyptian gods, so technically it's Egyptian, not Greek." Also evidence of how desperate my mother has been getting lately to find names that are versions of her own or Osiris's after having so freaking many kids. Two hundred years ago she wouldn't have touched anything even mildly Greek in origin.

But wait. Ry looked up what my name means? He can't have just known. That's something a friend would do. Right? Right.

A strange, muffled chirping sound goes off in the background, and I think nothing of it until Ry nudges me. "Is that your phone?"

"Oh, yeah." I frown, pulling it out. I'm still not used to getting calls. Then I see the caller ID and my stomach clenches. Speak of the moon goddess. "Floods," I mutter, hitting *connect*. "What?"

"Hi, Little Heart."

"Mother? The connection's bad. You need to speak up." I can barely hear her—her voice sounds weak.

"I'm sorry, dear. I'm so tired these days. You haven't emailed me."

I roll my eyes, grateful she can't see it through the phone. I wasn't allowed to roll my eyes at home. So I do it again for good measure. "I haven't emailed because there's nothing to tell." The phone hangs in dead silence for a few moments. Of course she'd call me and then not even talk. I should tell her I'm in a park with a Greek boy, eating Greek food. That'd get her talking. "Mother? You still there?"

"Yes."

There is something off about her voice, though. "Are you okay?"

"I don't know. Things feel different with this baby. Off. I wish you could come home and help me. But the dreams haven't stopped, and I won't place you back in harm's way."

I want to be annoyed at her for calling to make me feel guilty, but I really never have heard her sound like this. "What about Osiris? He needs to do more for you. And you should call your sister." Nephthys helped me out, and I think she knows most of the spells and charms my mother does.

"She's already here. She's been a great comfort and help, unlike Hathor, who won't even let Horus visit. She has been acting very strange lately."

"Well, I'm glad Nephthys is there. You're going to be fine. Right?"

"Oh, I am sure I will be. I don't want you to worry about me."

She's a goddess. How could I worry about her? I don't like hearing her sound so . . . normal, though. And I can't help but remember the twisted memories I've been dreaming, what happens to her in them. But no. She's *immortal*.

I've never seen her pregnant, is all. This must be business as usual. "Have Nephthys make you some of that honey tea. We still have all of the stuff in the pantry. I'll email you tonight, okay?"

"Okay. Good-bye, Little Heart."

"Bye." I slide the phone shut and sigh. I don't need to worry about her. She's a goddess. Her goddess sister is there helping her out.

"Everything okay?" Ry asks.

"It's fine."

He gives me this look that says he knows it's not and he wishes I'd tell him why. Then it relaxes and he leans back, a cocky smile on his face. "I know what you need. Come on." He takes my trash and throws it away, then we walk back along the harbor, lined on one side by old, slimy-green overgrown concrete holding back the water, and on the other by old, not-slimy people selling all manner of nonsense, mostly revolving around the idea that tie-dye is an acceptable vacation purchase. A massive aircraft carrier looms above us like a floating skyscraper. A few other ships bob gently just out of reach, all museums now, and then we come to a dark, weathered-wood restaurant built into the pier out over the water. It is positively crawling with people.

"Good food? I'm pretty full."

"Wait right here," Ry cautions solemnly.

Folding my arms and giving him a pointed look meant to let him know that I am nothing if not impatient, I turn and watch as bike taxis pedal by, their drivers chatting to each other in Eastern languages, mostly complaining about the heat that day and the customers who don't tip.

My phone buzzes in my pocket and I hold back a sigh as I pull it out, expecting my mother again. Instead it's a text from Tyler, asking if we're still on for a movie night tonight. I even manage to punctuate everything correctly as I tell her yes, and I'm excited to see her. We're still waiting on approval for the museum room, and our shifts haven't been matching up as often. I finish the text right when Ry comes out holding two cups.

"So," he says, beaming, "which flavor do you want? Bright-blue sugar, or bright-orange sugar? They had pink-sugar flavor, too, but it didn't strike me as your style."

I reach for the cup full of blue stuff. My fingers brush his and it makes me feel so strange I almost spill the cup yanking it back. "What are these?"

"You've never had a slushie?"

"Nope."

"Pretty much the best thing in creation. Take a sip. Go on."

I do, and tiny pieces of flavored ice run along my tongue and coat my throat with freezing sweetness until they settle in my stomach with an odd, burning sort of cold. I laugh, delighted. It was all I could do to persuade Isis to let me get a fridge and freezer for the kitchen when I redid it. She's still convinced that eating things colder than room temperature makes you sick. Ice was always out of the question. "This is my mother's worst nightmare! I'm drinking freezing-cold sugar and I'm with a Greek boy!"

Ry's face lights up, and we walk in companionable brain freeze along the harbor toward where he parked a few blocks away.

"Oh, hey!" He stops and pulls out his phone, then stands next to me and holds it away from us. "Stick out your tongue."

"What are you doing?"

"Taking our picture!"

"Why?"

"Clearly you are not on Facebook. This is what teenagers are supposed to do. We take pictures of ourselves."

"That's . . . fun?"

He laughs. "Just stick out your tongue."

Raising an eyebrow suspiciously at him, I do as I'm told, to see that my tongue is an unnatural shade of blue. He leans into me holding the camera out at arm's length and takes a picture of us sticking out our flavored-sugar tongues. He brings it back and shows me the picture and . . .

I look so happy. It's almost startling; I haven't seen many pictures of myself recently, but in the ones I have seen, I look . . . ah, floods, Tyler's right. I usually look angry. And if I look happy in this picture, Ry looks like a constellation of joy.

"Want me to send it to you?" he asks, and I nod. He

taps fluidly on his phone and I take the opportunity to walk a couple steps away from where our shoulders were brushing. "Oh, hey, that's right. Tyler wants to do movies tonight." He looks up expectantly, and his face is so open and happy that it hurts.

I spend a lot of time being angry. It's making me tired. I want to look happy like Ry all the time. "I'll be there."

"Great! I didn't tell you, my mom had the room entirely redone based on your advice. I wrote down everything you said. She thought it was brilliant. So you get to come and see the fruits of your genius."

"Did you do the popcorn machine?"

"First thing that went in."

"I wouldn't dream of being anywhere else."

And that's how, three hours later, I find myself snuggled into a couch in the dark in a room I designed, perfectly happy.

And that's how, three hours and fifteen minutes later, I feel Ry's hand slip into mine.

For that single second before I pull my hand away, before my brain and will and resolve kick in, it's like magic. Real magic, not the stupid blessed-amulet kind, not the using-the-right-words-that-Isadora-can-never-know kind, but electricity and butterflies and a feeling of everything in the universe suddenly lining up exactly so and opening up an entirely new way to see, to do, to *be*.

I yank my hand away. It's too much. I can't—I can't

feel this. I can't do this. I stand and flee the room before he can finish saying my name, run out of his house, start the long walk home with tears in my eyes.

Butterflies are stupid, fragile things that have beautiful and tragically short lives. Electricity kills people. I don't need a new person to suddenly spring up under my skin and push out who I was, who I've already decided to be. Those feelings have no place in my life and I will not let myself be a fool in love, with love, let it take over and destroy me.

Love isn't magic. Just like my family, just like my place in the universe, it's something that I can't keep, can't make last.

I would rather lose Ry before I ever have him.

I stand in front of the mural, glaring at the image of my mother leaning over my father's dead body as she lovingly puts all of the pieces of him back together so that he can be given life again.

"Isadora," she says behind me, but I don't turn. I won't. She keeps trying to talk to me, trying to explain, but I won't let her. I don't want to hear her pretend like she loves me, pretend like I am anything other than her clever solution to the problem of no more worshippers.

"Isadora," she says, and this time her voice is hard and sharp, making a headache blossom behind my right eye. Still I don't turn, so she walks around, putting herself between the mural and me.

"Please," she says, and the tone in her voice is something I've never heard. I've heard her be gentle and sweet, but she sounds almost . . . desperate. "Please talk to me. Please let me help you."

I take a step back, narrowing my eyes, and fold my arms across my chest. "I can't stop you from talking. But I never have to listen to you again."

Rage blazes in her eyes, but is quickly snuffed out by something deeper and sadder, something that, for a fraction of a second, makes me want to step forward and wrap my arms around her in a hug. Comfort her.

No. Why would I comfort her? I take another step back.

That's when I notice that the mural behind her has turned black. The history of my parents, the triumph of my mother—it's all gone, swallowed up in darkness. A figure blacker than the black looms up behind Isis, holds out arms, and wraps them around her in the way that I wouldn't.

It pulls her into the darkness, and I watch.

I just watch, too scared to move.

I do nothing.

Amun-Re, sitting at the head of the court of the gods, could not make a decision between Set and Horus. They fought bitterly for eighty years, with little ground gained. Gods took sides, but neither Set nor Horus was the clear winner of the throne.

Isis, well-known for her maternal zeal, had been barred from the proceedings. So she disguised herself as an old widow and asked for shelter in Set's home. Spinning a tale of woe for him, she spoke of her son's wrongful treatment at the hands of a usurper who stole his inheritance. Set, enraged, declared that such behavior was wrong.

He did it in front of the court of the gods, unwittingly condemning himself.

Clearly he hadn't yet learned the lesson I knew from the day I could walk: my mother wins every argument.

"DON'T YOU THINK HE'S HOT?"

"*I don't care if he's hot.*"

Tyler smiles smugly at me. "So you *do* think he's hot, you just don't let that influence you."

"I am holding a nail gun. Do you really want to keep up this conversation?"

She raises her hands in surrender. "We will continue when you are unarmed."

I glare, turning back to the plywood bracing frames I'm nailing to the wall. The most important parts of design are the ones people never see, and since we *finally* got approval, I've spent the past two nights awake calculating and recalculating and sketching and graphing.

Plus, no sleep means no dreams. No dreams means no worries. I am letting this room consume me and push out thoughts of everything else.

Including inky blackness swallowing my tragic past every night in my dreams.

Including sugar-colored tongues and easy laughter and blue eyes and Ry.

Especially Ry.

He *knew*. He knew how I felt about relationships, that I just wanted to be friends. And that's the worst part—I did want to be friends. More than I even realized until he blew it and we couldn't be friends anymore, and I actually miss him. But he ruined everything. He knew, and he ruined it anyway.

"Whoa, Isadora, the board is officially nailed." Michelle eyes my work with raised eyebrows. Okay. Maybe someone else should be in charge of the nail gun today. But it's so satisfying.

"I've been texting you all morning," she says. Even though she's been right down the stairs the whole time.

"My phone's dead." No phone, no infuriatingly chipper texts and messages from Ry asking to meet so he can explain. Phones let people be both lazy and intrusive. Really, they're a terrible invention. We should go back to messengers. Or smoke signals. Way easier to ignore.

"How close are we?" She surveys the room with a concerned look. Rightly so. I'm getting a little nervous about brashly declaring I could do this. I want to prove myself to her (and to me) so very badly. This is the biggest project I've ever undertaken, and I need it to work. I need to show I can do more than color schemes and furniture.

But with the approval delay, we had to start on the framework without blueprints, so until yesterday my prep was pretty much pointless. Once Michelle got me the room's actual schematics, I had to compensate with extra bracings because there weren't enough studs in the drywall to support the weight of the plywood sheets and drop ceilings.

The only one happy about this situation is Tyler, with her infinite supply of "If only we had more studs!" jokes. I set down the nail gun and, not even sure what I'm doing, wrap an arm around her side in some sort of approximation of a hug. "I'm glad you're here," I say. She's keeping me sane.

"Of course you are," she answers, hugging me back. "I just wish I were—"

"If you say 'studlier,' I'm kicking you out."

She laughs, and I go back to nailing. Opening night is in a week. Already announced to the papers, already sent out in the newsletter in fancy, glossy, full-color glory. Which means I have two days, max, to finish the framing—easily a week's worth of work—and then four days for drilling the star maps I've already marked on the plywood, painting, wiring, installing, and finessing.

Leaving me only one day—the day of the evening gala—to clean and get the actual exhibits set up.

It's impossible.

I will make it happen or die trying.

I don't realize I've said that last part aloud until I notice Michelle's horrified face. "We could use some help," Tyler says from the finished section where she's touching up the cement floor's black coat of paint.

"Not just anyone," I say. "You pull in, say, Lindsey from the front desk, and it'll take more time to explain what needs to done than it would for me to do it all myself."

"So we could use some capable help," Tyler amends.

Michelle bites her lip. "With the cost of the storage and extra security, we don't really have the budget for—"

"I can do this. Tyler is enough."

"What time did you get here this morning?" Michelle asks.

"Five," I say. Lie: I've been here since 3:30. After the attempted robbery, security confiscated keys from everyone other than Michelle, but she gave me the only

153

employee-held copy so I could drop off supplies and work whenever.

"It's four thirty. Have you taken a break?"

"I can't." I turn back to the wall and line up the gun with a new board. But when I pull the trigger, nothing happens. I pull it again and again. "*Floods*, what is—"

Michelle stands next to me, dangling the unplugged cord. "Lunch. Now. If you come back one minute before six thirty p.m., I will have security deny you entrance."

My mouth gapes open wider than a hippo's, but every line in Michelle's small body is rigid and unyielding. I could pick her up and deposit her outside this room, then lock the door . . . but I wouldn't put it past her to call security. "Fine," I snap. "I need to deliver paint samples to the guys doing the display stands, anyway."

"I'm going to smell your breath when you get back and I had *better* smell food!"

"That's disgusting!"

"I don't care!"

Tyler straightens and drops her roller.

"You"— I jab one long finger, the black polish sadly chipped, in her direction—"already ate lunch. Keep working."

My boots crack like a gunshot with each echoing stomp down the stairs and through the mostly empty museum. At the bottom I feel someone staring at me and whip around, ready to catch Tyler trying to skip out, but her angular frame is nowhere to be seen among the small group passing in a blur at the top of the stairs.

A strange smell dries and pricks at the back of my mouth; I can't place it, but it doesn't belong. It reminds me of the break-in at Sirus's house, which makes no sense because there isn't any salt breeze here.

I fight the odd urge to shudder, and stalk out of the museum instead. I can run three errands in two hours if I literally *run*.

Laden with bags, I drain the last of my Coke. I had three of them instead of anything to eat. It was faster and I couldn't get that dry sensation out of my mouth. Besides, Michelle'd have to stand on a stepladder to smell my breath, so I think I'm okay. Except it's 6:24 p.m., and I'm hovering outside the taped-up DO NOT ENTER signs blocking the wing-in-progress. She can't get mad at six minutes early. The plastic handles of the bags are threatening to tear and burning where they dig into my exposed forearms.

I duck under the rope as a ringing laugh echoes from behind the closed double doors, and a warm feeling instinctively rushes through me.

Then I realize who the laugh belongs to.

"Amun-Re, I'll kill him," I growl, kicking the doors open. Tyler doesn't even have the decency to look ashamed of herself; she's sitting in the corner on the floor, reading something out loud off her phone. Ry laughs again, not looking up from where he is paging through the plans. *My* plans. For *my* room.

I let off a stream of the foulest cursing I can think of, the Croatian rolling off my tongue as it usually does in times like these. "Get your hands off of my papers," I snap when I finally run out of names to call him. His smile has dropped away, and underneath his olive skin the blood has drained from his face.

Tyler's eyes are wide, but she still looks like she's enjoying everything. "Was that Arabic?"

"No, it was Elvish. What is he doing here?"

Ry shakes his head, as though coming out of a fog. "I'm helping."

"You are not—" My mouth freezes as I look around the skeleton of the room. Three-fourths of the bracings are up, perfectly placed. It is precision, quality work. When I left two hours ago, only a third of them were done, and I had been working since 3:30 a.m.

Oh, no.

"But . . . Michelle said they have no budget for help," I stutter.

"Volunteering," he says with that brilliant, dimpled smile. "Looks great on college applications."

"How did you—?" I put my hand against one of the bracings.

"Theater tech crew since middle school. I've built dozens of sets. Plus my dad is an artisan. I'm best with metal, but I should be able to handle all this work and the wiring."

The wiring. That's been my biggest concern from the beginning. I've never handled wiring in any of my designs, and even though I know how I *want* it to work, I've been sort of hoping that somehow it will work on its own. The special-ordered lights and equipment are sitting, perfectly boxed, stacked against the wall in my room at Sirus's house. I can't even look at them without feeling sick.

If the lights aren't perfect, there is no point to this room. If I blow this room, I prove to Michelle (and myself) that I can't handle big projects.

"You really think you can do the lights?"

"I'm sure of it."

I close my eyes and put a hand over my aching forehead. I don't want him here. He makes things weird and complicated and I hate that I have his face memorized, that I can recall exactly how his hand felt slipping into mine.

Because the worst part, the real reason I haven't let him call me, the real reason I am now terrified of him?

Part of me wonders how bad it would have been to let myself feel what I wanted to feel, and see where things went with letting him hold my hand.

I can't do that. I can't set myself up for loss. I can't want something that can never be lasting or real.

But this room is real, and, chaos take me, I need him.

"I own you," I say.

Ry's dark eyebrows rise in a silent question.

"For the next week you have no life outside of this room. I own your time, your brain, and especially your truck. You do exactly what I tell you to do without question. This is *my* room and you are only here as long as I want you to be. Understand?"

Ry nods, his smile sloppy with happiness that has no reason to be there.

"Good thing Scott isn't here," Tyler says, still texting. "He'd be totally hot for you after that speech."

"You." I point at her and she looks up, her expression exhausted. I soften my own and smile at her. "Go get food for everyone, because we're all going to be here for a long time tonight. Take my card, and take your time."

"Sir, yes, sir!" Tyler jumps up, mock-saluting. "I love it when you get bossy. It's kind of adorable." She rummages through my bag for my wallet and runs.

I take a deep breath and grab the next bracing. Ry is instantly at my side, helping me move it into place. His movements are strong and assured; Tyler and I fumbled through this together, neither of us particularly skilled. He holds the awkwardly long two-by-four in place while I position the nail gun.

He waits to start talking until I'm in a rhythm. "So." *Thunk.* "About the other night." *Thunk.* "I got the feeling—and correct me if I'm wrong because I don't speak

Girl, though I've tried desperately to learn it—that you were"—*thunk*—"a little upset." *Thunkthunkthunkthunk*.

"You're at least remedial level in Girl," I say through gritted teeth.

"What did I do?"

I turn to glare at him. He ruined everything, that's what he did! "What part of 'just friends' didn't you get?"

His smile is a masterpiece, a da Vinci study in innocence. But his blue, blue eyes spark with something else. "Friends hold hands."

"Oh, do they?"

"All the time."

"So you hold hands with Scott a lot, then."

"Had to quit. Sweaty palms."

"Tyler?"

"Too bony. Brought up childhood nightmares of dancing skeletons."

"Any other friends I don't know who you regularly clasp digits with in this apparently very normal aspect of friendship?"

"No, not really."

"So by 'friends' and 'all the time,' you mean 'no one' and 'never.'"

"Did I mention that English isn't my first language? Much like with Girl, sometimes the nuances elude me."

"Good thing you write poetry then."

He laughs, throwing back his head like the force of

mirth is too much for his neck to handle. It is an avalanche of a laugh, a zephyr wind that sweeps me back with its warm surprise, and I realize too late I am smiling and laughing with him.

Then his eyes meet mine and the warm desert wind zips away, leaving a vacuum in its wake, and there is no air in the room, no air between us, and I cannot look away. He leans in closer and his gravity-enhanced eyes flick down to my lips then back up to my eyes, binding me pulling me terrifying me.

"Isadora?"

"Yes?" I answer, but something's wrong with my throat and it comes out strange and breathy. Does my name always sound like music?

"Could you maybe not point the nail gun at my chest?"

And there's that air that was missing before. I thank the idiot gods for my dark skin as my face burns and I whip the gun back to the work that needs to be done. This room can't be finished soon enough.

"How do you do it?" I ask Tyler, not looking up from the neon manicure I'm giving her. She's spending the night so we can get an early start on painting the plywood boards tomorrow. And because Tyler convinced me we both needed a girls' night or she would lose her mind. I'm so tired I can barely see straight.

"How do I do what?"

"How do you love Scott?"

"Whoa, hate my boyfriend much?"

I look up, panicked that I've offended her, but she's still smiling. "No, no, that's not what I meant. Scott is awesome. I mean, how do you . . . how do you let yourself love something you know will end? Don't you feel sick all the time? Terrified? What will you do when you lose him? Even if you don't break up, you'll die. It won't matter in the end."

She takes the nail-polish brush out of my hands, screwing it back onto the bottle. "Isadora, sweetheart, that is the saddest thing I have ever heard. I don't say this lightly, because my mom is a therapist and she drives me nuts with the analysis, but have you considered therapy?"

I shake my head, avoiding her eyes. "I don't mean to be depressing. I just . . . I used to think I was part of something that would last forever, you know? And it didn't. And I don't want anything less than forever, because it feels so empty. I don't ever want to be used again."

She leans back against the edge of the bed and puts her arm around my shoulder, pulling me close. "I don't know about forever. It's not something that concerns me. And maybe Scott and I will get married and have fifty babies and be old and wrinkled together. Or maybe we'll crash and burn and break up, and if it happens it'll be devastating, but what we have now makes me happy. And I can live in that happy, and feel safe there, knowing that even if things change, I'll always have had this. You know?"

I nod my head against her shoulder, but it's a lie. I don't know. I wish I did.

The sky is achingly blue, the air achingly sweet, my hand achingly aching. I finish drilling the last of the stars on my section of the huge sheets of thin plywood that will be the new walls and ceiling. My stars are so accurate you could navigate a boat by them. Assuming you had a boat that needed navigating in the middle of an exhibit in a museum.

The sound of the drill whining higher and lower as Ry works on the already-marked pieces drowns out almost everything, including the laughter from the tarp by the pool where Deena, Sirus, Tyler, and Scott are painting.

I crack my neck, raising my arms straight up to ease the pain in my back from spending so many hours leaning over. It's been nice to work outside, at least, and I'm glad that Sirus and Deena have a big enclosed patio and pool instead of a yard.

Ry is both fast and accurate, and only a few minutes after I'm done, he's already finished with his much larger section. We walk over to the others to help there. So many things to do, still. I keep a running list in my head, going over it constantly. I will not forget anything. Everything will be perfect.

"Honestly? I don't get it." Scott holds up one of the

plastic pieces—one of a thousand—that will go into the drilled holes to secure the tiny lights. "These are black. So why are we painting them . . . black?"

"Different shades of black. They have to be exactly the same."

"I beg to differ on your choice of semantics." He adds another freshly painted piece to the "done" section of the tarp. "They do not *have* to be exactly the same. You *want* them to be."

Sirus laughs. "And what Isadora wants has to happen. You don't know her very well, do you?"

I resist the urge to glare. I'm trying not to be angry. So I settle for sticking my tongue out at him.

Deena slaps her husband's shoulder. "Hey, I admire a little perfectionism. I wish it would rub off on you in the area of, say, folding laundry."

"If you admire a little perfectionism, you must full-on worship Isadora," Scott says, "because this goes way past a little."

This time Tyler slaps Scott's shoulder, making his brush jump and smear black paint on his hand.

"Okay, that's all the sitting my pregnant joints can take." Deena pushes herself up with a groan. "I'm taking my mandatory Saturday nap."

Sirus follows her. "Duty calls. You know what they say: the family that naps together . . . ummm . . ."

"Gets the clap together?" Scott offers.

Sirus glares. "Do I need to ban you from my innocent baby sister?"

"No, sir! I meant, uh, gets to clap together. *To.* Not *the.*"

With a stern nod, Sirus leaves. I scoot into his spot, but the work here is almost done anyway, and we can't do anything else until these dry and we test whether it's better to insert them and then paint the boards, or paint the boards and then insert them.

"So, are you going to school here in the fall?" Scott asks, finishing his pile, then painting a streak on Tyler's pale-white arm. She keeps at her work, not even looking up.

"No, I already have my GED."

"You graduated early? Or, wait, is that a normal time to graduate in Egypt?" He puts a curlicue on Tyler's long, skinny bicep.

"I didn't go to normal school. Homeschool, I guess, though I was mostly in charge of myself." After I stopped wanting to learn the history of the gods, I set up my own course of study. I was quite rigid—I never wanted to be behind once I got out of my parents' house.

"Ah. Boring! No wonder you're willing to be friends with us. You don't know any better."

"I wish I'd been homeschooled," Ry says, leaning back and stretching his face toward the sun with his eyes closed.

"Why?" Tyler keeps painting, though Scott has now

started playing tic-tac-toe with messy black streaks on her bare calf.

Ry rubs the back of his neck, not looking at us. "Oh, you know. School can be . . . weird."

"How so?" All I know about American high schools is what I've seen in movies, and I doubt it's very accurate. Too many spontaneous, choreographed dances for real life. That or the American education system is seriously screwed up.

"Do you want me to finish yours?" Ry grabs for the rest of Tyler's nearly gone pile.

"Don't change the subject. How is it weird?"

"It's kind of embarrassing."

Tyler finally stops, leaning forward, the motion messing up Scott's attempt at an x.

"You made me lose!" He paints an angry streak through the tic-tac-toe game.

"Shut up. Ry is telling an embarrassing story."

"It's not a big deal. There was just this girl, who got kind of . . . aggressive?"

"You got beat up by a girl?" Scott's eyes light up with wonder and delight.

"No! She thought—do I have to tell this? We dated for a little while and then broke up, but she was really upset about it. It got so awkward I ended up eating lunch in the boys' bathroom every day for the last two months of school to avoid her."

"Oh, that's so sad!" Tyler says.

"Was she ugly?" Scott asks, writing his name beneath the tic-tac-toe board.

"No, just not my type. She was pretty enough. Kinda short. Blond. Very . . . orange."

Tyler finishes her last piece. "Fish-belly white is the new tan. But what *is* your type, if it isn't short and fake-baked?"

He smiles, not looking at me in a way I swear is so deliberate it feels like he is staring right at me. He turns toward Tyler while he leans in closer to me, his shoulder almost brushing mine. "It's a very, very specific type. And does not include the color orange."

Scott brings his paintbrush up to Tyler's face, tracing it along her jawline. "What's your type, Tyler?"

"Half-Taiwanese, obnoxious, and soaking wet." With a roar she grabs Scott under his arms, dragging him toward the pool. He stands and they wrestle back and forth until they both trip over the edge and fall in with a massive splash.

I watch them and laugh, loopy with fatigue and grateful that the tarp is far enough away from the edge that they didn't get it wet. Tyler and Scott scream, pushing each other under the water. "We'll have to have a pool party or something when we finish this," I muse, mostly to myself. I want to buy strings of lanterns to give Deena and Sirus as a thank-you gift. They'd light up this area so pretty at night.

"So, we're done here, right?" Ry asks.

I nod. "Thanks. You can go home. I'll call you when we're ready to paint more."

"Who said I wanted to go home?"

I notice the twist in his smile too late. With a roar of his own, far deeper than Tyler's, he throws me over his shoulder, runs, and leaps into the pool. I push him away, surfacing with an angry splutter as my hair funnels streams of water right into my eyes. Ry jumps up next to me, laughing as he shakes his head and sprinkles me more.

"You jackal! Why did you do that?"

He stops laughing and looks at me with utter sincerity. "You looked really hot. I thought this would help. It didn't."

"Ha. Ha." I hook my foot around his ankle, yank it out from under him, and shove his head under. When I finally let him up, Scott jumps on my back, screaming, "Boys against girls!"

Tyler jumps on Scott on my back and we all go under, Scott with a death-grip on my tank top. I finally wriggle away, surfacing for air with a gasp. The last time I was stuck underwater . . . I remember. The dream. But it wasn't a dream.

Isis had taken me to the banks of the Nile like she did most days. I was playing in the sand while she searched for whatever she needed to collect for our spells. A shadow blocked the sun and I looked up to see tall, tall Anubis.

"Hello," he said, with his sharp teeth.

"Hi."

"Do you know how to swim?" he asked.

"No."

"Well then, time to learn!" He picked me up and threw me straight out into the middle of the river before I could even process what was happening.

I sank. I'd never been in the water without my mother before, and she wasn't there, and I didn't know what to do without her. The water was murky and stung my eyes, but I knew if I waited, my mother would come for me.

She had to. She always came for me.

And when my chest hurt so much I wanted to cry and I couldn't hold my breath any longer, instead of inky blackness claiming me like in the dream, those hands I knew better than any others in the world grabbed me and pulled me up into the air.

It was the only time I'd ever seen my mother cry. I was upset and crying and she was, too, screaming at Anubis, who was laughing and telling her to calm down, it was all a joke.

That's why he was banned from our house! I can't believe I blocked that out. And I can't believe that when I next saw him, just before coming here, he genuinely didn't recognize me, didn't even remember what he'd done. That's how unimportant I am.

I wipe my eyes, stuck with so much remembering.

Funny how something can trigger a dead memory. I can still taste the water, still remember the grit it left on my skin, still remember just how sure I was as I drowned that my mother would not fail me.

I can't believe I let that nightmare replace the actual memory. My mother saved me. Of course she saved me. She would never have let something like that happen to me. She may have used me, may be replacing me now, but she took care of me.

I need to call her. I'll call her tonight, just to see how she's doing.

Someone laughs behind me, pulling me back into the present. I turn around to see Ry peeling off his shirt.

My traitor heart thuds. I am not thinking about the Nile, or Anubis, or calling my mother anymore. Because Ry isn't wearing a shirt.

It's just skin.

It's just skin.

IT'S JUST SKIN.

I'm so busy not noticing Ry's torso that Tyler tackles me from behind and I let myself sink to sit on the bottom. It's quiet down here, aside from the thrashing legs of my wrestling friends. And I can see clearly, though everything is distorted. It's nothing like the Nile. I can save myself now.

Then Ry sinks down, too, sitting next to me, his hair floating up all around his face as he smiles and winks. I can't look away from his eyes, blue even through the pool-filtered light.

Thud goes my traitor heart.

Thud goes my brain.

Thud goes Scott, pushed down next to us as Tyler dances on his shoulders, finally breaking the spell of those ridiculous blue eyes. I surface for air.

I feel like I'm drowning again.

Isis still wanted more power. She continually feared for Horus's safety, and she envied Amun-Re his distance from the worries and strife of the other gods. And so she watched, and waited, and found the perfect method of poison delivery.

One day as Amun-Re walked the earth, a snake bit him. But it was not a snake he had created, and so he could not name it and remove the venom. Amun-Re, god of the sun, was dying.

He called on Isis, possessor of great magic and also renowned for her medicinal skills. Isis was waiting, as she had been since she put the snake in his path. She would heal Amun-Re in exchange for his true name—a name she could call on to use his power.

Amun-Re listed name after name, trying to confuse her, but she would not be deterred. And, knowing Isis, Amun-Re feared that telling her his name would be telling Horus his name as well. And, knowing Isis, Amun-Re did not doubt she would let him die.

In the end, he had no choice.

My mom would have let the sun die before she'd let Horus come to any harm. And yet I got to decorate my own tomb.

"RELAX." RY LEANS AGAINST THE CHIPPED
Formica counter, the long, lean lines of his body showing the relaxation he'd have me imitate. "We're ahead of
schedule. We can't install the lights until the paint is completely dry on everything anyway."

I nod, twisting our receipt between my fingers. It feels
weird to be out, getting dinner instead of having Tyler or
Scott drop it off for us. But Ry has a point—we *have* to
wait. And thanks to his work the last four days, we can
afford to.

That, and if I lose any more brain cells to paint fumes,
I might not remember my own name.

Tyler had been very excited to get the afternoon off,
and even more excited when I gave her Sirus's tickets to the
Padres game to take Scott out to. They deserve a fun evening together, and Scott's obsessed with baseball, which
Tyler inexplicably thinks is adorable. I couldn't handle the
idea of the crowds. A quiet evening with Ry was far more
appealing.

Ry hands me a cup filled to the brim with Coke and
ice. "You need this."

"Floods, yes. Thank you."

"We're doing great." He nudges me with his elbow,
and I smile into my cup. "You've totally earned tonight."

"But did we have to come here?" I'm not a snob, and
Ry has taught me that the best regional food is usually
found in the sketchiest-looking places, but this run-down

hole-in-the-wall Mexican eatery is not looking promising.

"Trust me. Once you've had carne asada fries, you will never go back. It's like a burrito threw up on a plate of cheap french fries."

"You do realize that's the least appealing description of anything, ever."

"Patience, young grasshopper. Soon you will understand."

The girl behind the counter leans up to the open window between the cash registers and the kitchen area to grab our food. "That boy is the most beautiful man I have ever seen," she says in low, sweet Spanish to the girl handing forward the containers.

The girl in the kitchen smiles, her dark eyes flashing. "Should I have messed up his food so he'll have to come back to the counter?"

"Yes! I want to look at him more. Is it too late?" Her hands hover over the Styrofoam lids, like she doesn't want to commit to handing us our completed order.

I snort into my drink, choking as the carbonation goes down wrong. If only Ry knew what they were saying. I get hit on, sure, but it's nothing to what Ry has to deal with on a daily basis. The more I'm around him, the more I realize he wasn't actually exaggerating.

The counter girl looks at me nervously. "Can I get you anything else?" she asks in English.

I answer in Spanish. "No, thanks, but if you want, we

can sit where you can see him better."

"Your, uh, boyfriend?"

"Oh, no. He's a friend. But it's okay to look at friends, right?"

She grins at me and nods. "Come back again soon," she says, in English, with a lingering look at Ry.

He's been staring studiously out the front window the whole time. "Hey, I forgot my notebook at the museum. Okay to eat there instead? We can have a picnic."

"Sure." I grab utensils and shoot an apologetic smile at the counter girl as we walk out into the warm, ocean-heavy, late-afternoon air.

"You speak Spanish?" Ry holds my door open as I climb into his truck, and he hands me the food.

"Oh, yeah. Very well-rounded homeschooling."

"Hmmm." He closes my door and gets in on the other side.

I have a rather horrid thought. "Do *you* speak Spanish?"

"I speak Greek, English, Arabic, and a little bit of Girl."

Relieved, I rest my head against the seat, the food's heat almost uncomfortable against my thighs. Then I realize he didn't actually answer my question. "*Hablas español*," I say, glaring at him.

He grins but says nothing.

"You jerk!" How does he speak so many languages? Apparently the chatter about the American school systems is wrong. They are seriously doing their job.

"Hey, it's not my fault you all chose to talk about me in a language you assumed I didn't speak. Which, in this area, is a very unsafe assumption since most everyone speaks at least a little Spanish."

"But you encouraged the assumption!"

"I didn't want the cashier to feel awkward. Plus now I know you're okay with the fact that I really enjoy looking at you."

"I am—you're not—that's *not* what I said."

"And I quote: 'But it's okay to look at friends.'"

I will not blush. I will not blush. I will not blush. "I can engage in a clinical assessment of physical features. It's possible to recognize attractiveness without being attracted."

"What is wrong with being attracted to someone? It's a natural thing."

"Yes, well, cancer is a natural thing, and we try our best to kill it."

"You're comparing love to cancer. I don't believe it."

"Actually, we were talking about attraction. And you proved my point about avoiding attraction because you jumped straight from there to love. But yes, love as cancer holds up quite well. Something that grows inside of you against your will and without your consent, slowly taking over more and more vital parts until it kills you. That fits nicely." I smile, pleased.

"Stop," Ry says, frowning. A deep crease forms between his eyebrows. "That's not funny."

I'm taken aback. I talk a lot of crap to Ry—especially the last few sleep-deprived days working so closely together. Usually he laughs. Oh, no. Oh no. "I'm sorry. Have you lost someone to cancer? That was really insensitive of me."

"No, it's not that. It's just—you can't *really* think that about love. Not really."

I shrug, an itch growing between my shoulder blades, soul deep. "It makes everything hurt more," I finally say as we get out of the truck, because it's the only true thing I can think of to say about love right now, here with Ry. If I hadn't loved my parents—I mean, come on, I *literally* worshipped them—finding out they were just using me wouldn't have been so awful.

We stop at my favorite tree beneath the footbridge and Ry climbs under the stairs and into the roots. I follow and we open up our food without a word.

Except . . . oh, idiot gods, why didn't you choose this area of the world for your sad little reigns? Because carne asada french fries are, beyond a doubt, the most deliciously disgusting thing I've ever tasted in my life. I shovel them into my mouth, cool sour cream and guacamole, crisp salsa fresca, mushy fries, melted cheese, tender meat. Every bite is like a revelation of what the perfect harmony of ingredients can be.

"I think they modeled this stuff after ambrosia," Ry says, watching me with a tentative smile.

"I can feel it clogging my arteries as I eat. And I don't care. It's going to be such a happy death." I finish before him and lean back against the roots, groaning and holding my stomach. "Too much. Not enough."

He laughs, and I stare at the bits of sky bold enough to break through the dense, tangled weave of branches. I should have brought mints. My throat prickles with dryness, a strange, salt chemical taste that sucks the moisture out, leaving my tongue thick and chalky in my mouth.

The back of my neck tingles and I look around sharply.

"Something wrong?" Ry asks, wiping his mouth with a napkin.

"Do you smell something weird?" I don't see anyone, but I can't be *this* paranoid. There has to be a reason it smells like Sirus's house did the day of the break-in.

"No, why?"

My phone rings before I can answer him. Mother on the caller ID. The ancient Egyptian in me wonders if the strange smell and fear are connected to my mother somehow, connected to the twisted memories I dream every night.

"My mom. Gotta answer."

"No problem. I'll go get my notebook and be right back." He grabs our garbage and leaves. His limp has an odd grace to it, almost like a swagger without the

177

arrogance. I love it—it's enough of a break in his physical perfection to make him interesting where otherwise he'd be unreal.

Oh, floods, I am *not* watching him walk away.

I answer the phone with a distracted, "Hey."

"Little Heart," my mother says, and she sounds tired. Maybe that's a normal mom thing, but Isis the Ever Energetic doesn't do tired. Now I'm worried again. In her emails she said Nephthys has been staying with her around the clock. I wish I could be there, too. No, I don't.

"What's up? Are you okay?"

"I have not been well. But I'm feeling better. How are you?"

"Better is good. I'm fine. Busy."

"That's nice. Your work is going well? Your friends are kind?"

I've been trying to tell her more about my life in my emails. It feels . . . nice. Nice to be able to talk with her a little more. She never listened to me when I was at home, but she can't very well ignore typed words she has to respond to. "Yeah, everything's really good."

"I am glad. I wanted to ask your opinion on colors for the baby's room. You're so much better with this than I am."

I sit up straight. "Yeah, sure. What are you thinking?"

"I need something neutral, but I want it to be warm and welcoming. Maybe blue and yellow?"

I bite my lip, running through palettes in my head. "You don't want to do a baby's room in yellow—it's not soothing enough. Brown and green will give you more options if it's a girl and you want to add some pink accents. If you go with a spring green, it's still a very warm color without the inherent energy of yellow."

"Yes, I think you're right."

I smile. She really does value my opinion on this stuff, just like she told Michelle.

"Also, how many coats do you think we'll need to cover up the black?"

"I would say—wait, the black? What room are you painting?" My heart skips erratically. She wouldn't. She *wouldn't*.

"Your old room."

"MY ROOM? You're painting over my room for some stupid baby?"

"Isadora! I didn't think you'd mind. I have always used this room for babies."

"I spent months decorating! It's MINE. Of course I mind! Do you even care that I'm gone? Obviously you don't think of me at all! I knew Osiris didn't, but at least you pretended to care." I stand, livid, almost screaming into the phone. I know I'm not going back home, but *she* doesn't know that. How dare she destroy my work, give my place in the family *and* my room to my replacement.

"That's enough!" The whipcrack of her voice makes

my temple throb even over the phone. "If I'd known you would be so selfish and immature about this, I wouldn't have brought it up. I'm very disappointed in you. You know your room is temporary. It isn't the room that will matter in the future, and I don't see you putting time and care into that one."

"My—Amun-Re, Mother. You really think it's okay to destroy the one thing that was mine because I still have my *tomb*? You really can't wait for me to die, can you? It's amazing. It's absolutely amazing that the goddess of motherhood can suck *so bad* at being a mother! Well, guess what? You can give *both* rooms to your new victim, because *I am never coming home*. Ever. EVER!" I scream the last word and throw my phone down, wishing she were here so I could hit her, physically hurt her to make her feel what I'm feeling, to finally show her what she does to me on the inside.

And then somehow my rage is leaking out my eyes and I sit back hard onto the roots, my tailbone stinging, and dig my knees into my eyeballs as I wrap my arms around my legs.

I hate my parents. I hate them. And I hate that I hate them, because it means I care. I wish I could feel the same way they obviously feel about me—I wish they were the nothing to me that I am to them.

Ry's arm around my shoulder is surprising; I'm still not used to being touched, and it's comforting. "Is your brother here?" he asks. "I thought I saw him."

I shrug, not lifting up my head. "Maybe. He's been paranoid lately. I can't remember if I told him I'd be here tonight or not. I'll text him and tell him I'm coming home now."

"I have a better idea. Text him and tell him you'll be home late. I know where we need to go."

The Milky Way is above me, each star a perfect point against the black night sky. I had gotten so used to San Diego's light pollution that I'd forgotten just what, exactly, the stars were supposed to look like.

But even as I drink them in, let them fill me while the desert night air tickles my skin, I can't help but notice something is off. They don't anchor me like they used to. They're still mine, my soul still sings to see them, but . . . I don't know. That invisible something, that heartstring that used to stretch between me and my guiding stars is different. It's shifted, and I don't know where or why. Maybe it's because Orion—the stars Orion—isn't out?

I wiggle my legs, trying to ease my spine off a raised groove in the metal of Ry's truck bed.

"I should have brought pads or something," he says from where he's lying flat on his back next to me.

"No, this is perfect."

We drove straight east, where the sprawling tangle of the city suddenly ended in nothing. Through and over a mountain with wind turbines so big it looked as though the gods from one of Ry's myths set them there. Then back down the mountain and past kilometers and kilometers of horizon-meltingly flat farmland to the waves and crests of sand dunes in the middle of nowhere.

Though the air still tastes different, the sand and the stars surround me like a blanket of home, a snatch of comfort and familiarity in the middle of a strange new land. And Ry found it for me when I needed it the very most.

I turn my head and look at his dark profile as he studies the sky—his long, straight nose, angled jaw, full lips. He could be a Greek statue come to life. I smile at the thought, and a small line in my chest, the line that anchors me and connects me to my Orion, suddenly gives me a tug.

Toward *this* Orion.

I close my eyes and hold perfectly still. The impulse to scoot over and close the gap between our bodies, to rest my head in that spot between his shoulder and chest where I know—I know—it will fit perfectly, to twine my fingers through his—

I don't want that. I won't. I can accept that he is important to me. He's a friend. I'd had no idea how much I needed friends until Tyler and Ry. And I'm vulnerable right now, still trying to find *me* in this new place, still trying to fill the holes inside. I can't seem to keep my heart from leaking out of the cracks, like sand clutched in a fist.

But I won't fill those holes with him. I can't. To do that

would invite other holes to be punched in right next to the ones my parents made.

I will fill myself with the desert and the sky. I will be stone and stars, unchanging and strong and safe. The desert is complete; it is spare and alone, but perfect in its solitude. I will be the desert.

I open my eyes to see Ry staring at me, and my desert soul erupts with turquoise water, floods and cascades and waterfalls rushing in around my stone, swirling and eddying around my rocky parts, pushing and reshaping and filling every hidden dark spot.

"Stop it!" I gasp.

"What?"

"That thing you're doing! With your eyes!"

"Um, opening them? Or blinking? Should I not blink?"

"Just—make them less blue or something."

He laughs, oblivious to my drowning desert. "It's pitch-black out here. You can't see what color they are."

"But I still know, and they know I know. So just— point them somewhere else."

He blinks, slowly, the line of dark lashes standing out against his skin in a semicircle smile, mocking me before he opens them again. "But it's okay to look at friends, remember?"

"Shut up." I smack my hand against his chest and then it stays there and I need to pull it back I can't leave it there why isn't my arm pulling it back and oh idiot gods I can feel his heart beating and nothing has ever felt so simple and pure and honest and right in my entire life.

GET OUT OF HERE, my brain screams. Move your hand, Isadora. Move it. Move it. But that line, that traitorous anchor that misaligned, that picked the wrong Orion, it's singing out to stay.

Ry reaches up, ever so slowly, and puts his hand over mine and now his heartbeat is underneath it and his skin is on top of it and I can't breathe, I'm holding my breath because if I let it go I have to make a choice to drown or to flee, and I cannot make this choice

I like the person I am with him

and no one's skin has ever felt this way before

and every part of me—*every part*—is in those few square inches of palm and finger connected to him

and I am going under

and I don't care

"Isadora?"

My name in his voice sends a jolt through me, creates me in the way he sees me and feels about me and the way I would be with my name in his mouth forever. Finally I understand the power in names, the power that we give people when we tell them our names.

"Orion," I whisper, and he is. Orion. Forever now, *he* has replaced my Orion stars in name.

He lifts his free hand toward my face, turning on his

side to close the distance between us and—

I panic. I have never been so terrified in my entire life. This is a beginning and that means there will be an end and I can't, I can't have something that feels this way end.

"I can't." I sit up, pulling my hand from his. It's cold, so cold, colder than the rest of me and I want to hold it myself to try and get back that sensation but I cross my arms over my chest instead, cut off the errant line connecting me to him. "I'm sorry. I don't want to do this. I can't. Please take me back now."

He looks like he has something to say, but I stand up and jump over the side of the truck bed, then sit in the passenger seat. After too long Orion—*Ry*—gets in and starts the truck.

I will not drown tonight.

I will not drown ever.

I am the desert. I am the desert. I am stone.

Set and Horus continued to challenge each other in the courts of the gods. They fought in ludicrous displays of strength and cunning—including a spectacular event that involved seeing who could stay underwater as a hippo longest. That one resulted in my mother's decapitation.

It didn't stick, obviously. Gods are awfully hard to kill.

In the end it was Osiris who put an end to the contests between Set and Horus, threatening to drag everyone into the underworld if they didn't cease fighting.

My father's equivalent of "Knock it off or you're all grounded."

WE DRIVE IN SILENCE UNTIL THE MOUNTAINS loom dark and swallow us into their winding embrace.

"Can't or don't want to?" Ry says.

"What?" I ask, my forehead against the glass of the window. I'm trying to pull the smooth chill into my head, let it flush out the water sloshing around in my soul.

"You said you can't, then you said you don't want to. Which is it?"

"Can't. Won't. Don't want to. It's all the same thing. Let's don't talk, okay?" If cutting off a beginning hurts this bad, I can't imagine what ending something later would do to me. I just want to go home and go to sleep.

Too bad sleep isn't very comforting lately.

"No, they really aren't the same thing. If you don't want to—I mean, genuinely are not attracted to me, do not think of me that way, cannot stomach the thought of touching me—then I would understand and I would never press the issue again. But that's not how you feel."

"How do you know?" I snap.

"Because I'm very pretty."

I whip my head around to glare at him; he's smiling like he couldn't be more amused. "You aren't *that* pretty."

"I am to you. So let's establish that it's not that you don't *want* me to kiss you senseless. It's the idea of being senseless that terrifies you."

"You are unbelievable."

"I am, aren't I?"

"Unbelievably arrogant."

"Not arrogant. Confident. There's a difference."

"Which you clearly do not understand. But again, it doesn't matter what my reasons are, because they're mine and they aren't changing. So you can be my friend, or you can get out of my life."

"Hmm." He raises his eyebrows, noncommittal. "What did your mom say?"

"What?"

"This afternoon, on the phone. What did she say that upset you so much?"

"None of your business."

"*Friends.* It's my business when someone makes my friend cry. I'm worried. Is she . . . did you come here because you weren't safe with her?" He asks gently, like one would talk to an injured animal, his tone raising the question he doesn't know how to phrase.

"No! Not like that. She sent me here because she was worried about me."

"Tough love?"

"No, she was worried something terrible would happen if I stayed in Egypt. She . . . she's kind of a mystic? And she was having bad dreams. That sounds stupid."

"No," he says thoughtfully. "I get that. I think people pay less attention to dreams than they should. We get all sorts of signals and information from our environment that our brains can't process, so our subconscious does instead."

"You think bad dreams are a legitimate reason for making huge choices?"

"Good dreams, too. Good dreams especially. Don't you?"

"No." I pause, thinking of all the dreams I've had lately. The dreams of darkness swallowing and unmaking everything around me while I . . . do nothing. Do I really feel guilty that I don't worship my parents like they want me to? I didn't think I did. I thought all I felt about that was anger. But . . . "Maybe. I don't know. I hope not."

"Okay, don't get mad, but it sounds like your parents care. They're trying to keep you safe in the best way they know how."

"No, that's just it. They *don't* care. This was an easy solution for them, so they took it."

"Why are you so sure they don't care?"

"I can't explain it. It wouldn't make any sense to you. But trust me. My dad's whole job, his whole life is taking care of people, and he's so consumed by it he doesn't even know who I am. He doesn't even live in my world. And my mom, she's like this legendary mother figure, but when it comes down to it, she doesn't actually care about me. I'm a means to an end. Period. They don't love me. They never have."

"I don't think you know what you're talking about when you talk about love. How do you define it?"

"Well, according to you, I wouldn't know."

He smiles. "My family has made a special study of love. It's kind of our thing. Did I ever tell you my mom is a professional matchmaker?"

Of course she is.

"Anyway, we Greek poets think a lot about love, too. We finally went ahead and made three separate definitions and words for love just to try and explain it. So maybe—maybe your parents love you in a way you don't understand, or a language you don't speak."

"That's crap, Ry." I speak every language in the world.

They don't care about me in any of them.

"Okay, maybe they don't love you in the way that *you* need. But I can't imagine that they don't love you at all. That's not possible."

"You don't know them. They're capable of anything." Adultery, blackmail, attempted murder, having kids just to create more worshippers. What's not loving one stupid, noncompliant mortal daughter on the list of their sins and shortcomings?

"No, I mean it's not possible not to love *you*. Even if they are the worst parents in the world. If they didn't love you, you wouldn't be here."

"Whatever," I mutter, grabbing his phone to find some music so that hopefully he will stop talking. He doesn't know them. He doesn't understand. He can't understand. If even Sirus doesn't get it, Ry never ever could.

I scroll through the playlists and stop. "Why do you have a playlist named 'Isadora'?"

He snatches the phone from me with a sheepish grin. "In the interest of not pissing you off anymore tonight, let's not select that particular playlist." Ignoring my glare (why oh why couldn't I have inherited the instant-headache glare?), he turns on something instrumental. "So, if you could reconcile with your parents and get what you need from them, would you be willing to date someone? Is that the hang-up?"

"What's the point of it all? Love sets you up for

disappointment and pain, and we all end up alone one way or another. Nothing—*nothing*—in my life can last."

"I take issue with every aspect of that. Love is a point in and of itself. But the core of your argument is that relationships are pointless because they don't last, right?"

"Sure."

"Then why do you design rooms? I mean, they're nice now, but styles and tastes change. You aren't creating anything permanent. The museum wing you're killing yourself for will only be there for a few months. So what's the point in spending so much time and energy investing all of yourself into something that isn't permanent?"

"That's different."

"How?"

"Well, for one thing, rooms don't betray you. I've yet to meet a room that snuck around and slept with its sister-room's husband."

Ry snorts. "Well, most people won't do that, either. And unlike rooms, people can give things back to you. Contribute as much or more than you do."

"People aren't like designs. I can't pick and choose everything that goes into them, and I can't imagine anyone picking what I am."

"You have a terrible imagination then. But what I'm getting is that this is a control issue. You're scared because the other person is outside of your control, and so is the way they make you feel."

"This is a terrible analysis. Designing is nothing like love. Idiot gods, you must be the worst poet *ever* if these are your metaphors."

He laughs. "See? How could I ever be arrogant with you around? Someday I'll let you read my poems and decide for yourself. But I'm not backing down on this. Are you a coward?"

"*No.*"

"So stop being such a wimp about the potential for pain. If that's how you're going to live your life, you may as well be an empty room yourself. I like you. I want to be your friend, but I also want you in ways that are very much not just friendly. And I'm not going to apologize or pretend I don't."

I tip my head back and squeeze my eyes shut. Why is he forcing me to address this? We were fine. We were doing fine. I liked what we had. It was *safe*.

He pulls to a stop and I'm shocked to see we're already back at Sirus's.

"I get that you're scared and that you've been hurt. But doing what is easy and safe is no way to live, and a life without passion and love is so far beneath what you deserve."

His words hit me in the gut and my head spins. He's right. I've been choosing alone because it's safe and easy. It doesn't mean that I'm stronger or smarter than everyone else. Just that I'm . . . scared. I'm letting all of the hurt I've had over the last few years keep me from moving forward.

I climb out robotically as Ry opens my door, avoiding his eyes. I *am* a coward.

"I hope you have good dreams tonight, Isadora," he says, and the way my name leaves his mouth, it sounds like I should be as strong and brave as I used to think I was. It sounds like the part of myself that I left locked in my tomb isn't as buried as I thought. It sounds like there's a possibility for an Isadora who is strong and brave without being hard and closed off. Who is strong and brave and hopeful and open. Who is lovingly optimistic and forgiving.

It sounds terrifying.

I want to hear it again.

Sirus is on the couch when I drift inside, confused and exhausted.

It's the middle of the night, but he's sitting there folding pieces of clothing so tiny they can't possibly be for a person, even a baby. He smoothes the wrinkles out of a creamy-white satin blanket, the look on his face a combination of wistful and tender.

I lean against the wall, so tired I want to sink into it and sleep forever. I have to be at the museum in three hours. I have to see Ry again in three hours. I don't know what I'll do. Tonight feels like it changed something. Maybe everything. Maybe nothing.

Sirus looks up and smiles at me.

"How can you love it already?" I ask. "The baby, I mean. You don't even know what it is, much less who it is. But you love it."

He pushes his thick-rimmed glasses back up where they slipped down his nose. "I don't know. It's funny, isn't it? But I think Mom was right when she told me I'd have no idea how much she loved me until I had my own."

"Floods, please don't ever let me utter the words 'Mom was right.'"

He laughs, and I walk the rest of the way into the room and curl up on the couch, staring at the floor.

"You all right, kiddo?"

"How are you okay with our parents? How can you be okay with them after what they did to us?"

He lets out a long breath. "You mean the death thing."

I wipe under my eyes. Ry's words echo through my head, that maybe they do love me, just not the way I need. "How can they love us if they'd let us go like that? Shouldn't they want to keep us forever? They could. I know they could. Stupid Whore-us is immortal, and Anubis. Why did they change the rules? Aren't I—aren't we good enough for them?"

"Oh, Isadora." He sits next to me and puts his arm around my shoulders. "Didn't you ever let Mom talk to you about it?"

"I've spent the last three years trying my best not to talk to her about anything."

194

"You should have let her explain. She talked with me about it a lot. But I guess I never had the shock you did. You assumed immortality from all the stories. I kind of assumed I'd drop dead at any time, but it wasn't a big deal to me."

"How is death not a big deal?"

"Because it's not the end. We have this life, we make it the best we can, and then we discover the next life."

"Mother never did. Why should we die when she doesn't?"

"Did you ever wonder why none of us live nearby or visit often?"

"Because Mother's a crazy control freak and you couldn't wait to get away."

"No. Because when we were old enough, Mom felt like she had given us all the tools she could to have happy lives, and she wanted us to do just that. Live. Make our own mythology, not be swallowed up by hers. Live the kind of happy, drama-free, painful and joyful mortal life she couldn't, and at the end of it come home to be ushered into our next life by the two people who brought us here in the first place. I know you think mortality is evidence that they don't care, but giving us the ability to grow and change and progress and then *finish*? That was the greatest gift two ageless, eternal, very very stuck gods could think to give the children they love more than anything."

"If mortality is such an awesome gift, why does life hurt so much?"

"Maybe because you're doing it wrong?"

I look up, glaring through my tear-matted eyelashes, and Sirus laughs.

"Am I scared of the horrible things I know will happen to my kid to hurt him? Absolutely. But would I stop those things at the risk of taking away joy and growth and the absolute embracing of life? Never. Because I love this child for being mine, but I also love him for being who he will be, and I can't tell you how excited I am to watch him discover that for himself."

"Or herself."

"I, uh, may have peeked during the ultrasound. . . ."

"Deena will kill you."

"Which is why this is our little secret. And also can I say, after spending the last few weeks with you, I'm more than a little relieved my new guy won't have girl hormones?"

"No, you cannot say that unless you want to get the beating of your life." I punch him in the shoulder for good measure, then stand to go to bed. I'm as confused as I ever was; things still feel like they're slipping down a muddy landslide slope in my soul, my desert hopelessly destroyed, and I don't know how the geography is going to change when everything finally settles. I hope it settles soon. "So you really don't think they had us just to worship them."

"There are plenty of other, far easier ways to find worship. They had us because they wanted us. Because they love us."

I sigh. "You know, life was a lot easier last month when I could hate our parents and be violently opposed to the idea of romance."

"Heh, yeah, it—wait, romance? What is—"

"Good night!" I run upstairs and collapse into bed, but Sirus's and Ry's words spin in my head, swirling and shifting the parts of me I thought were immovable. And the clock counts down to my next meeting with Orion.

Ry.

Orion.

*O*rion's stars swirl and dance above me, winking an invitation to join them. I lift my fingers, trailing them through the warm black of the sky, leaving a ripple of sparks like water disturbed. The stars remain just out of my reach, every inch of my skin tingling in their light. There are two new stars, two stars such a perfect and brilliant blue they make an ache flare in my heart. I am hurt and broken, but in these two perfectly blue stars I dare to hope.

My mother has her own constellation, a new one, and it is beautiful though it stirs my rage that here, too, she is eternal and immortalized and I am left on the ground, left to live on it and eventually sleep under it.

Then I notice there's a section of the sky, not dark but empty, not a glimpse into the eternities, but an endless hole in the sky. It surges forward, swallowing my mother's stars one by one.

I watch.

No. I will not watch anymore. I have watched this happen time and again, and this time I will not. "Stop!" I scream, punching my fist upward to make it change course.

It does.

It covers my hand, crawling down my wrist, along my arm. It is cold, and hot, and neither. It makes me want to shake out of my own skin, to run screaming, to curl into a ball and let it overtake me, uncreate me, scatter everything I am and could be into the cosmos to feed its own endless entropic hunger. It is despair.

There is no one to help me, no one to protect me. I will be undone, and then it will finish its work on my mother's stars.

I've failed.

At last the gods were settled, formed into the roles they would have until they fell out of power and out of memory. Osiris, god of the underworld. Isis, dominant queen of magic and motherhood. Horus, god-king of Egypt. Hathor, boozed- and sexed-up wife. Set, tamed god of chaos. Nephthys, companion to Isis. Anubis, assistant in the underworld. Thoth, gentle god of wisdom. Others lost along the way, their dominions taken over by stronger gods. But such is the nature of time.

The kingdom developed, left behind constant strife and conflict. And with movement came a gradual fading. A slipping away, as people moved on from the turbulent, violent eras that required turbulent, violent gods.

And Isis proved, yet again, her fierce adaptability to any situation. Some women have babies to save marriages. My mother started having babies to quite literally save the lives of her family.

"NO, NO, NO NO NO NO NO," I MOAN, GRABBING fistfuls of my hair and staring up at the new ceiling. We planned meticulously for overhead lights, and they hang perfectly, spotlighting where the freestanding pedestal pieces will go. The stars installed perfectly. Even the electrics have all worked. But I had counted on the lowered ceiling resting against the tops of the new walls and blocking out the light and . . . it doesn't.

They match up. Almost perfectly.

Almost.

Almost perfect takes this room from awesome to amateur.

Little cracks of light seep through here and there from the now-blocked windows, and it makes the whole thing look cheap and thrown together.

"We'll fix it," Ry says.

"Yeah, it won't be that hard. Right?" Tyler answers, her voice drifting on into almost a plea at the end.

"We can't do it. We have to be done in twenty minutes for the moving guys and security to come install the pieces. Only Michelle and I can be here while they do that, and it will take them until tomorrow morning to set it all up and get everything wired for alarms."

"So that gives us eight hours until the gala?" Ry asks. "We can do a lot in eight hours."

"That's assuming they get it done in time. And besides, I need those hours to fix whatever the movers screw up, to deal with anything that might need last-minute attention! All that time you bought us, Ry." I shake my head, feeling sick to my stomach. It was going so well. "It was for emergencies. It gave me time to deal with emergencies."

"Well, say hello to your emergency." Tyler squints

upward. "We could line it with black electrical tape or something?"

"You'll be able to see it. If we caulk it and then—"

Ry shakes his head. "It'll never dry in time to paint it."

"What if we do the tape and then paint over it?" Tyler says, walking into the middle and swinging her arm in an arc over her head. "If we do a smooth line of black paint, you won't be able to see the tape, right?"

I bite my lip. It's not a permanent solution. If any of the walls get shifted, it could rip away and damage the paint underneath, causing an even bigger problem. And it'll be a nightmare working in here tomorrow, because everything will be set up and we won't have much room to maneuver, and we'll have zero room for error with the paint.

"It doesn't have to last forever." Ry puts a hand on my bare shoulder and I close my eyes at the sensation of his skin on mine, momentarily lost in the heat and feel of him. *Amun-Re, focus, Isadora.* "It can be good enough for now, and if we have to fix it later, we fix it later."

"I don't like good-enough."

"Good-enough can always be made better. Later. Right now we're going to take good-enough and we're going to be happy about it."

I nod, not missing the fact that his hand is still on my shoulder. All day we've worked side by side, and he hasn't pushed anything from last night. But his eyes seem bluer, and I can't ignore that even disasters feel more manageable with him here, and when he's next to me, my traitor body reacts in ways that I definitely did not give it permission to. I don't know what to do with these feelings or where to put them or if I want them or why I should or why I shouldn't.

It's been a complicated day.

"Good-enough is good enough." I take a deep breath. "I have to stay here to make sure they put everything where it's supposed to be. You two be in charge of getting tape?"

"Me! Me! I want to be in charge of tape on my own." Tyler bounces up and down on the balls of her feet, her shoulders twitching to a beat I can't hear.

I smile. "Okay! And it's a good idea, too. I never would have thought of it. You're brilliant."

"All my ideas are good, Isadora." She looks pointedly at Ry's hand and I want to shrug it off I'm so embarrassed, but then that would mean I actually noticed and cared that it was there, and . . .

I don't know. I don't know what to do, and it's driving me crazy. Grinning, Tyler runs out past us, leaving us alone. In the room. Alone.

"I was thinking last night," Ry says.

Yeah, I was, too. So much I thought my brain would pop. But I have no conclusions, and I don't want to know what he was thinking about. But I really, really do. Chaos take me, I kind of hate him. "Oh?"

"You know the story of Persephone, right?"

Ooookay, not what I was thinking he'd be thinking about. It wasn't Greek mythology keeping *me* awake. "Um, yeah."

"I was thinking about framing, and how so much of what we think about our lives and our personal histories revolves around how we frame it. The lens we see it through, or the way we tell our own stories. We mythologize ourselves. So I was thinking about Persephone's story, and how different it would be if you told it only from the perspective of Demeter versus only from the perspective of Hades. Same story, but it would probably be unrecognizable. Demeter's would be about loss and devastation. Hades's would be about love."

I frown. "Yeah, I guess I see what you're saying." I just don't get *why* you're saying it, you psychotic, maddening boy.

"It's all a matter of perspective. And maybe we thought we were living one story, when if we look at it a little different, we can reframe everything—all our memories and attributes and experiences—and see that we're actually living a different story."

I cross my arms and shrug out from under his hand. "Are you lecturing me again, Orion? Is that what this is?"

He grins, white teeth blinking their innocence. "I would never dream of lecturing you. I just thought it was interesting to think about."

"Mmm-hmm. And how many times did you practice

how you'd phrase this little gem of wisdom when you told me?"

He runs a hand through his thick, dark curls. "Ah, umm . . . who says I practiced it?"

I raise a single eyebrow at him.

"Two. Maybe three. Five. Not more than five."

My phone rings, and Ry looks relieved. "I've got to go before they start unloading the stuff. Plus I am so far behind on my poetry it's not even funny."

"It's kind of funny, actually," I say, before answering my phone. I wave to Ry as he leaves, my heart doing a weird, not entirely unpleasant flippy thing as he smiles, then say, "Hello, Mother."

I don't know how to feel about talking to her, not after my dreams last night and my conversations with Ry and Sirus. Maybe I really have been framing my entire life wrong. Maybe she isn't a villain. Maybe I've been too hard on her.

"Isadora, you're coming home. Right this instant."

Then again . . .

I wave frantically at the short, stocky man with a bushy mustache wheeling in a box. "There! No, not there. There! Under the large light. Yes. And the narrower pedestal goes immediately opposite."

"Stop ignoring me, young lady!"

"I'm not ignoring you, Mother." I step aside as they use a dolly to maneuver another huge crate in. "I am, in fact, doing the job you made me take."

"No. Go back to Sirus's house right now; he'll book a flight for you. Today. Immediately."

I roll my eyes, then shake my head at the poor mover who thought I was annoyed with him. "I'm not coming home today. Why are you freaking out?"

"The dreams changed last night. You were in them again. Something happened, something changed to make the darkness focus on you, too."

I shudder involuntarily, remembering my own dreams. She is right. Ever since I came here, my dreams have been about her in danger, not me. What changed?

Oh. I'd actually cared this time. *I* changed. I didn't stand by and watch my mother get eaten by darkness. But if I admitted to her that I had the same dream, I was admitting that they were real. And I wouldn't put it past her to get the embassy involved. Send someone to kidnap me and forcibly bring me back. Come here herself. . . .

And there's another shudder. My mother, here. Talk about a nightmare. "No, Mother, listen." I weave through the wooden crates and men coming in and out of the room until I get out into the hall to a quiet corner. "I've been thinking a lot lately. About a lot of things. And . . . it's good for me to be here. I'm not ready to come home yet."

"I thought you said you were never coming home again," she says, her voice edged with both anger and sorrow.

"I know. And to be honest, I meant it. But now . . . I

don't know. I'm still figuring it out, and I need time. Plus I have worked my freaking butt off on your exhibit and I am not leaving before I finish. Besides which, no one from Egypt knows where I am—only Sirus does, and you know I'm safe with him. I think I'd be in more of this mysterious danger if we were together. So"—I take a deep breath— "I'm asking you. *Please.* Let me stay."

She's quiet on the other end for a long time. Too long. "I think that's the first time you've sincerely asked me for anything in years." She sounds like she's on the verge of tears, and suddenly it hits me how much the last few years must have hurt her, too.

This is stupid, and hard, and I hate it. I hate Sirus and I hate Ry and I hate having to change and realize that I was wrong. Being wrong *sucks.* "I know, Mom."

"Okay. You can stay to open up the exhibit. But I want you back as soon as I have this baby. Then I won't be vulnerable anymore, and we can get to the bottom of this together."

"I'm . . . I'm really happy here, though. I'd like to come back again."

"We'll talk about it—Isadora! There's a boy, isn't there?"

"What? I—no—I didn't—no, there is no boy!"

I can feel her smug smile through the phone. "Is he kind? Does he come from a good family? Does he treat you well?"

"*Mother.* I have to go. They're bringing in your bust and I'd hate for them to damage it." Actually maybe I can convince them to accidentally knock off one of her nipples. Preferably both. "We'll talk later."

"Very well. Be safe, Little Heart."

I almost hang up, but I pause. "You, too."

A crash and a litany of swearing from the movers saves me from the helpless feelings welling up in me. Work now. Emotions later.

The next morning Ry texts me at six a.m. to come down and let him in. I've been at the museum all night, touching up paint where it got dinged, adjusting placement, and so on and so forth. It's not easy working with this junk, either, because even though I know we've got a ton exactly like it at home, here it's all invaluable, *priceless* junk. So everything had to be done in gloves and with the utmost care, under the watchful eyes of two security guards.

I push open the back door and Ry's there, illuminated by the pale morning light and the overhead lamp that hasn't turned off yet. He's wearing a blue sweatshirt jacket with the hood up, and it makes his eyes an impossible color. If I were an artist, I'd spend all day mixing paints trying to capture it. If I were a normal girl, I'd want to lean forward and trace my finger down his face and get lost in that blue.

Oh, idiot gods, this is what lust feels like. I guess I finally understand.

"I thought you'd need this," he says, holding up a bottle of Coke.

Now I *really* want to jump on him. I am in so much trouble, and, honestly, I don't know if I care anymore. I'm feeling braver by the hour. "Thank you," I say, taking it and not minding that my fingers trace against his as he passes it to me.

"I also have the tape. Tyler said she'll be here later because she has to stay after and set up the hospitality tables, so she won't have time to go back home and change."

"Ah. Well. Bad news is that we now only have until ten a.m. to make any adjustments. We have to be out by then so they can finish connecting all the alarms and go through a few test runs of the system."

"Chug that Coke and let's get to work, then."

We spend the next four hours in a flurry of activity. Fortunately we're both tall enough that we can use a smaller ladder to seal the line between ceiling and wall, but even that takes a lot of creative stretching since several of the pieces are flush against the wall. It takes us longer than it should to get the tape exactly right since we have to work together instead of at opposite ends of the room like I'd planned.

For the last corner, I have to stand on the top of the

ladder and stretch, without putting any weight on the false walls. Ry puts his hands on my waist, steadying me, and I realize I am not afraid of falling.

Maybe he was on to something with those decorating metaphors, after all.

I smooth the last piece of tape, and luck is finally with us. The room is dimly lit enough at the top that by the time we finish taping, it's almost unnoticeable. You'd have to be looking for it. With the setup drawing all eyes to the display pieces, I doubt anyone will.

"We don't need to paint," I say, laughing and giddy with relief and exhaustion.

"Should we turn off the extra lights and flick the stars on? See how it looks?"

We've got floodlights in while we're working, which will be out of here in a few hours, and we haven't seen the full effect yet. But . . . I don't want to.

"Let's wait. I'd rather see it for the first time tonight. Besides which, if there's something wrong, I can't fix it. I'd rather not know."

He laughs. "It's going to be perfect. It's amazing."

I smile and nod, examining the room one last time, envisioning what it will look like when the drop cloths are taken off the exhibits and all of the effect lighting is on. It'll work. It has to.

"Now I'm taking you home so you can sleep and get ready before your big debut."

I don't argue. Every part of me aches, and if I don't get a nap before tonight, I'll be dead on my feet. I want to enjoy this. We walk out, closing the door behind us and nodding at the security guards.

"Hey!" Tyler waves, coming up the stairs and meeting us halfway. She's wearing sleek black pants with red heels and a white button-up shirt, her hair pulled into a tight, high ponytail. She nods toward the guards. "Tweedledee and Tweedledeelicious up there permanent fixtures?"

"Yup."

"Wait, are you done?"

I nod, the prospect of my bed calling and making my brain heavy and slow. "Done."

She squeals and throws her arms around me. "I didn't think you'd do it."

"And I appreciate your confidence."

"Well, okay, I'm stuck for the day. I'll see you tonight?"

I hug her tighter. "I needed you, and you were here for me every step of the way. You are amazing. Thank you."

"Hush. Don't make me get all weepy when I put on makeup for once." She pushes me away.

I wave and turn to finish going down the stairs.

"Oh! Also, there was some guy asking for you at the front desk when I walked in, but he left when they said you weren't available."

"He was asking for *me* me? By name?"

"Yeah."

"Sirus?"

"Uh, I know what your brother looks like. It wasn't him. Dark guy, like Sirus I guess, really tall, handsome in kind of an intimidating way."

I frown. "Doesn't ring any bells." It's odd, and I get that sensation that I can't quite swallow again. After tonight, I actually might go home like my mother wants me to. Something is wrong, and I don't know what, but I know that my mother will be able to figure it out.

Until then, I'll try not to worry. There are a lot of people in and out of the museum today who would know who I am or need to talk to me—delivery people, security guards, and so on and so forth. Still, walking out I'm glad Ry is next to me.

I walk into the exhibit. Everything is dark; not even the stars are lit. All the pieces are gone save one: a statue of my mother in the middle of the room, lit from within.

I don't remember that statue. It's not supposed to be here. Where are the murals? Where are the stars? Everything is wrong! The whole thing will be a fiasco, and I'm going to be so humiliated. I've ruined it all.

Then I realize it's not a statue. It's actually Isis.

"Mother?"

She smiles, holding one hand out to me. "Hello, Isadora."

"You came for the opening?" I feel a brief burst of pride and happiness, then embarrassment. "The room isn't supposed to look like this. I did a better job—I did—I don't know what happened."

"You changed something," she says, her voice soft and sad.

My hand flits self-consciously to my hair. "Oh, I, umm . . ."

"In the dreams. In the darkness. You changed something."

"I couldn't let it—I can't just watch anymore."

"You know I would rather you be safe," she says.

I open my mouth to argue, but . . . I do know. She would rather be undone a thousand times than let something happen to me. This is her truth, my truth, the truth I pushed away and buried under all those years of anger and misunderstanding.

"I love you," she says, a single tear tracing down her skin.

"Mom, I'm so sorry, I—"

But it's too late. I was right all along. She's nothing but a statue, and as I watch, she crumbles into dust. I'm left alone in the dark.

Isis became what she needed to be. She used magic, and cunning, and sheer brute force of will to protect her own. She survived. She evolved, usurped other gods' roles, took worship wherever she could get it, and made it sustain her.

She transcended generations, transcended cultures, spread her influence and worship past the borders of the plot of earth and sky that gave birth to her. She carved a huge sphere of worship and power, and then she carved a tiny, deeply protected bubble to feed herself and those she loved. She would change, she would diminish. Still, she would last forever.

But if we learn anything from my family, it's that sometimes even things that last forever don't last forever.

DON'T PANIC. DON'T PANIC. IT'S GOING TO BE OKAY.

I emailed Mother before we left, finally giving her the actual details of my dreams. It's close. Too close. I take deep breaths, looking at myself in the sun-visor mirror of the car. I manage not to look terrified, which is good. "Sirus, can you help me book a flight home?"

He stops at a light, glancing at me incredulously. "Really?"

"I want to come back here. I mean, if it's okay. But

something bad is coming, and . . . is it weird that I'm worried about Mother?"

He smiles. "It's a little weird, yeah. Mom can take care of herself. But I know she'll appreciate it. And of course you can come back. We can book a round-trip ticket, if it'll make you feel better."

I smile. It does make me feel better. Everything will work out.

As Sirus's car goes over a speed bump, I put in my other earring, the beaten gold discs hanging down and tickling my neck. The earrings match my belt, square pieces of linked gold resting along my hips, and my trusty gold sandals complete the accessories. I wanted something for my wrists, but nothing felt right.

And . . . I'm wearing white. It's a sleeveless dress with a draped cowl-neck. The hem sweeps the floor, but with a slit that traces up to my midthigh. My mother gave it to me for my last birthday, and I've never worn it. I threw it into the suitcase on a whim when I was leaving; I never wanted to put it on because I thought I'd look like Isis. With my jewelry and kohl-rimmed cat-eye makeup, I do look like an Egyptian goddess. But I look like *myself* as an Egyptian goddess, which feels fitting tonight.

"I'll be back in an hour with Deena," Sirus says, pulling to an illegal stop in front of the museum. Deena hasn't been feeling well; she took today off work, which apparently never happens. "We can't wait to see what you did."

He smiles proudly, and I smile back. "It'd better be good, though, considering you've been so busy that you haven't done a thing on the nursery."

"Last time I checked, I still have a month." I cringe. Not if I go back to Egypt. "Well, I have good help. We'll get it done."

I get out of the car and take a deep breath. Throwing my shoulders back, I march up the stairs and knock on the blue doors, locked until the invitation-only opening gala starts. One of the security guys opens it, and his eyes go wide before he steps to the side to let me through.

I walk past the open entry and up the red stairs. Tyler squeals when she sees me—she's putting the finishing touches on the tables lining the walls. They're covered with white tablecloths, and several have bartenders behind them lining up bottles of wine. The nitpicky part of my brain thinks they really ought to have rich, dark beer if they want to celebrate ancient Egypt, but I suppose it's not as classy.

"So . . ." Tyler waves her hands at the tables. Each one has a tall stone vase of reeds on either end.

"Perfect! You nailed it."

"Have you seen the room yet?"

"No! Have you?" My stomach twists with nerves.

"No one has."

I take a deep breath, then scrunch up my nose. "We should wait for Ry. We couldn't have done this without him."

"Don't let him hear you say that, or he'll never let you live it down," she says, her eyes twinkling as she looks over my shoulder.

"It's true. He was amazing. If it—" Suddenly it hits me what she must be looking at that is so entertaining. "I take it back. It was all me. I let you and Ry help out of the goodness of my heart. I would have finished days ago without you two getting in my way."

"Is that so?" Ry says, and I turn around. I'm glad I've already steeled my face into a mock scowl, because otherwise my jaw would drop, and that would be inexcusable. He's in a deep-blue dress shirt, top button undone, and black pin-striped slacks. No one should be able to look equally good in jeans and a tee as they do dressed up.

"You look," he says, his eyes drinking me in the way I want to drink him in, "absolutely amazing."

I smirk. "You look rather pretty yourself."

"And Tyler looks devastatingly gorgeous," Tyler says. "Why, thank you, Tyler!"

I rip my eyes away from Ry and tug Tyler's ash-blond ponytail. "That goes without saying. I love your hair like this, by the way. Now let's go see our room."

I take a deep breath and then open the double doors wide. The floodlights are gone, and the room is completely black save for the light seeping in from behind me. "Here goes," I whisper, reaching down and flipping the switch on the power strip hidden next to the door. Tyler draws in a sharp breath and I close my eyes, waiting just a few seconds before I straighten and open them.

The stars glimmer around us, creating the illusion of space in the darkness. The displays are each bathed in a warm glow, standing out like islands of light in eternity, just how I'd envisioned.

Ry slips his hand into mine and squeezes.

I squeeze back.

A throat clears behind us and I whip around to see Michelle. She's staring at the room with a grin on her face, but a tightness around her brown eyes warns me that there's something wrong.

"What?" It's not the room. It can't be the room. Amun-Re, the room is perfect. She has to think the room is perfect. We pulled it all off, in record time, and it looks amazing. She can't hate it. She can't.

"We have a problem," she croaks. Her voice is tortured; it sounds like sandpaper scraping along her vocal cords. "I can't do the tour for the guests."

Tyler holds her hands up in the air like someone has a gun on her. "I can't! I haven't practiced anything! Oh, gosh, I'll end up babbling and saying something completely inappropriate and forgetting everything I ever knew about ancient Egypt. I'm forgetting it all even thinking about doing it. I'll quit right now before I'll ad-lib a tour."

Ry's hand is still in mine, and something about the skin contact and the completely irrational and inexplicable electric current it's sending buzzing through my body makes me feel buoyant and invincible. I was supposed to drift on the edges tonight, but it's still my night, and I'll own it.

"I can do it."

A little over an hour later, and the bravado I felt volunteering has collapsed and sits sour and flopping like a dying fish in my stomach. I'm in the hall corner outside of the still-closed room, leaning against the wall, looking at all the *people*. There are so many people. Why are they here? They shouldn't be here. This is going to be a disaster. Why do I even need to talk? Surely the room speaks for itself.

I wish Michelle hadn't told all the bartenders that Ry, Tyler, and I were too young for drinks. I hate wine, but anything sounds like a good idea right now.

"Hey," Ry says, and I startle, unaware he'd made his way through the crowds to stand next to me. "Nervous?"

"No," I say, but it comes out a whisper.

"You'll be brilliant. I know it. I've got a present for you."

I raise an eyebrow, glad to have something to focus on other than my impending embarrassment. "Oh?"

"I didn't have time to wrap it, but . . ." He reaches into his pocket and pulls out a gold cuff bracelet, open on a nearly invisible hinge. It's been etched with a design— scarab beetles, pushing the sun around the edges—and an oval jade stone in the center has raised gold around it to make it into the body of a scarab. He takes my hand and slips it over my wrist, closing it with a tiny snap. It fits like it was made for me.

"Scarabs," I say, unable to take my eyes off it.

"Yeah, I know they're bugs and that's weird, but I thought because of what they symbolize—"

"Hope and rebirth." I trace my finger along the smooth, cool jade, then look up into his eyes. "It's perfect."

"Yeah?"

"Yeah."

His smile is sunshine, and he reaches up and traces his fingers along my green stripe. "Plus it goes with your hair."

"You thought of everything."

"You're pretty much everything I've thought of for a while now."

My heart flutters and I have no idea how to respond to that, or to this gift. That same giddy current has resumed its path of havoc through my veins. "Orion, I—"

Michelle taps a glass and croaks that the room will open now with a special tour from the designer and daughter of the collectors. She gives a slightly painful preamble about ancient Egypt and its invaluable place in history, and the Egyptians' science and culture. And then she stops and I realize it's my turn.

Before I can talk myself out of it, I go up on my tiptoes

and kiss Ry's cheek, then dart past him so I can't see his reaction.

I stand in front of the still-closed doors. "We can learn the most about a culture by studying what was important to them. And in the world of ancient Egypt, they worshipped life and death in equal parts. Isis and Osiris, the focal points of our exhibit, represented those opposite"— I pause, realizing I mean what I'm about to say—"but equally beautiful and necessary parts of the human existence." I open the doors and walk in.

Everyone follows, crowding the doorway, the silence either awed or bored. I really, really hope it's awe. Standing in front of the first item, a remarkably well-preserved sculpture of my mother with the Pharaoh Thutmose II as a baby on her lap, I say, "I give you Isis, Mother of the Gods, Light Giver of Heaven, Mistress of the House of Life, Lady of the Words of Power. Goddess of Motherhood, Magic, and Fertility. First daughter of the Earth and Sky. Protector of beginnings." I pause, then smile. "Perhaps the greatest evidence of Isis's magic, however, was her breasts' ability to remain so round and perky after nursing hundreds of pharaohs."

There's a pause, then Scott, standing in the front row, bursts out in raucous laughter, which quickly spreads through the room, and I know I have them. Thank you, maternal nudity. Who knew you'd save me? Sirus, near the back with Deena, rolls his eyes at me with a grin.

I move to the next exhibit, a statue of my father, with the atef crown and his crook and staff, sitting in his throne. It gives me an odd pang of homesickness. "Isis isn't complete without her husband and counterpart, Osiris, Foremost of the Westerners, Lord of the Dead, Lord of Silence, Lord of Love. Osiris was the god of the underworld and afterlife, but unlike many cultures' underworld deities who lorded over damned and trapped spirits, Osiris was also celebrated as the god of reincarnation. His domain was one that was carefully planned for and optimistically anticipated."

I move to a large vase depicting both of them, my mother with the cow-horn headdress and huge, outstretched wings, my father with green skin, the color of rebirth. "Isis's motherhood and fertility ushers in life, and Osiris rules over the transition of that life to a new one. They are birth and death and rebirth, an eternal cycle, each incomplete without the other." I smile. "Of course, like all couples, they had speed bumps: arguments over whose turn it was to wash the pottery; Osiris leaving his crook and staff by the foot of the bed where Isis was constantly tripping on them; that time Osiris sired Anubis with Isis's sister Nephthys, the wife of Set. Families are complicated, and ancient Egyptian deities were no exception."

I gesture to a fresco on the wall of my mother, again with the cow-horn headdress, standing next to Whore-us in all his falcon-headed glory and the sun god Amun-Re.

The fresco is covered with elaborate hieroglyphs. I realize with a start that they are in my mother's own hand, her secret writing. She made this one herself. It's all I can do not to reach up and trace the words.

Idiot gods help me, I *miss* her.

"Horus, a miracle child conceived after Isis brought Osiris back from the dead, took his father's place as the god-king of Egypt. He was his mother's pride and joy. She even went so far as to poison the sun god to trick him into revealing his name to her, forever giving herself and her son power over the most powerful god. It takes the concept of an overcompetitive soccer mom to a whole new level."

I smile and wait for the laughter to stop. "So imagine her despair, after everything she did to get Horus here and then secure his place among the gods, when he married Hathor, the goddess of sex and beer. You thought your daughter-in-law was hard to get along with. . . ."

It continues like that, as I detail the story of my family, mixing mythology with the personalities the audience has no idea these gods have. I even use dear old Thoth's story of how he added extra days to the calendar to trick the Sun into letting the Sky have her children. By the end I am both exhausted and elated. As I discuss the murder of Osiris and make a joke about the rather overwhelming depiction of the vital manparts Isis magically made out of clay for the resurrected Osiris, I feel a strange sense of tenderness toward my parents. As screwed up as they are, I can't deny the impact they had on an entire culture. It's an impact that even thousands of years haven't been able to erase entirely. Somehow, talking about their dual roles has helped me reconcile my parents with their godly attributes.

And then I'm done, and everyone is applauding and breaking off into groups to look at the exhibits, and I watch it all with glowing pride, knowing that I made this room, but my parents made the stories that filled it. Even if I won't last forever, I'm still a part of this because it's a part of me.

Sirus and Deena walk up. "It's like you really know them!" Deena says.

Sirus and I laugh. She gives us a strange look, then sways on her feet.

"You look exhausted. Go home. Ry can give me a ride when everything's done." I hug them both and send them on their way.

Speaking of Ry . . . I look around the room, grateful yet again that being tall gives me a good vantage point. How do short people ever find anyone in a crowd?

I see him in the corner, talking with a couple. The man is hard-looking, all blocky features like he was clumsily and carelessly carved out of rough limestone. It isn't until he walks toward me and I see his limp that I realize he's Ry's father. Which makes the woman his mother. She turns and I stare, slack-jawed. Scott and Tyler weren't kidding—she is the single most beautiful woman I have ever seen. She has Ry's same dark hair; it trails down her back in thick, luxurious curls. All the parts of her that should be curvy are soft and perfect, and the parts that should be small are almost exaggeratedly so. Her bust in their entryway couldn't even begin to do her features justice.

I feel ragingly inadequate being in the same room as her. But then she takes her husband's arm in her own and smiles at him, and it's so obvious that she loves him—completely—and somehow that makes me feel better. They walk up to me and I have no idea what to say to them. What do I say to them?

"This is lovely," Ry's mom says, smiling. She is why the Greeks wrote poetry.

"I couldn't have done it without Ry. Thanks for letting me steal his time this last week."

She laughs, and Ry's dad twists his features into a smile. He's not handsome, but he's so solid, and there's something about his face that is both powerful and kind. I like him already. There's something familiar, comforting about both of them. Maybe just because I've been in their home and now it makes more sense.

"He's never been happier," she says.

"Oh, hey." Ry stands to the side of us, fidgeting, like he doesn't want me to be talking to his parents. "Umm, Mom, Dad, didn't you have that thing to get to?"

They laugh, then hug Ry, and we exchange good-byes. As they leave, his mom turns and makes eye contact with me, giving me a secret smile. That must be where he gets it. Curse those secretive dimpled genes!

Everyone gradually filters out, with many handshakes and congratulations, and even a business card from a real estate agent and an offer to dress houses she's trying to sell. Tyler and Scott head into the hall with Michelle to supervise the table cleanup, and I look across the starry eternity room to see Ry there, beaming at me.

We walk toward each other, meeting in the middle. Screw it all. I want this. I want him.

"You did it," he says.

"We did it," I answer.

I throw my arms around his neck and press my lips against his, and they are warm and soft and answer mine immediately. A thousand feelings burst through me, feelings I never wanted or even knew existed, and I am floating in the stars with Orion. My Orion. I want more more more of him, I want to map out a new chart of stars in my soul, stars that let him in.

I kiss him, and I am reborn.

Finally we pull apart, arms wrapped around each other. "Orion," I whisper, his name a love song and a hopeful prayer.

"Isadora," he says, "I have been waiting to do that for years."

"What do you mean, years? We just barely—," I start, and it's only then that I realize he said every word of that sentence in a different, obscure language. Languages he couldn't possibly know, languages that no normal person would even know existed, much less be able to speak. Unless . . .

Chaos take us all.

Osiris was murdered. Horus was poisoned by a scorpion. Amun-Re was fatally bit by a snake. The gods could die. The gods did die.

But Isis, the Great Lady of Magic, was always around to fix it.

Without Isis, even a god could die forever.

"NO," I WHISPER, BACKING AWAY FROM RY.

"I've wanted to tell you! And now—well, here. I have something to read to you." He pulls out a thin sheaf of folded paper from his pocket, face flush with excitement. And he's saying all of this, everything, in ancient Egyptian. The language my mother used to sing me to sleep. The language *no one* knows how to speak.

Floods. *My family aren't the only gods.* The world has shifted, tilting on its axis. This changes everything I thought I knew. And if he can speak in tongues . . .

Oh no. Oh no oh no oh no. Ry is a god. *He's a god.* It can't be possible. There aren't any others. My mother would have told me. She always said the other mythologies, the other stories . . . she said they were cheap copies.

Does she know there are other gods out there?

Not out there. Right here. And he knows who I am.

"How long?" I whisper.

He looks up from his papers. "What?"

"How long have you known? Did you find me on purpose?" I remember with icy clarity what he said to me after I got my hair cut—that he recognized me. He was looking for me.

His smile finally drops off as he notices my expression. "No, I—"

I laugh bitterly. "Gods. Just can't help yourselves, can't ever leave me alone. You set me up." Then I remember what little I know about the Orion from Greek mythology.

He's known as the Hunter.

My stomach drops and I stumble back, away from him. Every dream I've had screams through my head. What if the threat *wasn't* in Egypt? What if it was always here? All this time he spent worming his way into my trust, all those times he tried to get me talking about my parents.

All these feelings I was ready to have for him.

No. I stand straight, my spine a steel rod. "I don't care who you are or how long you've been alive or how immortal you think you are. I will *kill* you before I let you hurt my parents."

His treacherously beautiful face is white with shock. "Please, let me explain, Isadora!"

"Don't you dare use my name."

"I'm not Orion! Not the original one, anyway!" He runs his hands through his hair, voice tight with desperation. "He's long gone. My parents—they named me—my dad knew him and—look, I'm just like you! I'm seventeen! *I'm* not a god. My parents are."

The impossibly beautiful woman who specializes in love. The man with the limp who works with metal. No wonder they felt familiar. It was because they reminded me of my own family. "Aphrodite and Hephaestus."

"Yes! And I didn't mean to lie to you. I've waited so long to finally meet you, and I didn't know how to say it! How do you tell the girl very literally of your dreams that you're the son of ancient Greek gods?"

"You knew what I was."

He shrugs guiltily. "Not at first, but I figured it out. When you swore at me in Croatian."

"How do I know? How do I know any of what you're saying is the truth? Amun-Re, my mother was right. You really can't trust the Greeks." I back away from him, putting more space between us.

"Please, wait. Let me explain! I *was* looking for you. But not for whatever you think I was. I've . . . augh, this isn't how I wanted to tell you. When we talked about dreams, I was serious. I've dreamt of you. Every night. For years. I always knew you were out there for me, and every night I'd see you, made of stone, the strongest and

231

most beautiful girl I'd ever seen, and I'd speak to you in poetry and breathe life into the stone until it warmed and colored and you were there, and—" He puts his hands over his face. "I'm screwing this all up. The day I saw you with your hair short, I realized who you were. That was the best day of my life because I'd finally found you. And now . . . This isn't how it was supposed to go. I'd never hurt you. I *love* you."

My stone heart crumbles, the dust filling my lungs, choking me and making it impossible to breathe. He's lied to me this whole time, and now this? "You love me because of stupid dreams? You don't even know me! I trusted you, *Orion*." I spit his name like a curse, and it doesn't taste like hope and potential on my tongue anymore. "I have no idea who or what you are. But I swear to you I meant what I said. If you or any one of your cheap imitation gods comes near my family, I will feed your heart to Ammit the Devourer myself."

His eyes are a picture of anguish. I pull the stone pieces tighter around my heart. I will not break, not here, not now.

I turn and walk out of the room of my heritage, my past, and leave the boy I wanted to give my reborn future to standing there, alone. Fighting back tears, I run down the stairs, through the main entrance past a shocked Tyler, and out into the night. The park is empty save for the homeless who pepper the sidewalks, already asleep beneath tattered blankets.

I find the huge tree next to the stairs and climb into the roots, wanting to sink into them. My heart is not stone. My heart is sand and Orion's cruel tide has washed it away from me, scattered it, lost it.

Hands shaking, I pull out my phone. My mother needs to know about this. She needs to know there are other gods out there, and that they know about us. This must be it, it has to be it. The threat behind everything.

"There you are," a knife-sharp, guttural voice says, and it's only then that I finally place the salty, swollen dryness at the back of my throat that has plagued me.

It tastes like an embalmed body smells.

"Anubis," I whisper, and look up to see his jackal eyes glowing in the dark. "What are you doing here?" I didn't think anything else could shock me tonight, but the sharp canines Anubis flashes in a smile prove otherwise. "Did my mother send you?"

"Isis doesn't know I'm here."

"If she didn't send you, why are you—"

"Soon enough." He reaches down and takes my phone, crushing it between his powerful, paw-like hands. "Don't want you calling Mummy and ruining the surprise. Now, I have been in this soulless country far too long, and tonight I'll get what I came for. Hathor was wrong—your existence *isn't* entirely pointless."

He wraps his hand around my arm, pulling me up so hard I gasp in pain.

"Isadora?"

We both turn. Tyler's on the bridge, leaning over and squinting down at us in the dark.

"Are you okay?" she asks, her voice tentative.

Anubis squeezes harder, whispering low in my ear. "Do you know what I did to that driver? I embalmed his organs while they were still inside him. If you value your friend's life, tell her to leave."

I swallow hard against the panic welling up inside me. I will *not* let Tyler get hurt. "I'm fine."

"Who is that?"

"My brother," I stutter. "Half brother."

"Oh." She sounds dubious.

"He's giving me a ride home. I'll see you tomorrow."

"Okay." She hesitates. "Good job tonight."

"Thank you." I barely manage to push out the words, my throat so dry from Anubis's smell.

She lingers as if torn for a few achingly long seconds, then waves and walks toward the parking lot. Anubis drags me up the wooden stairs and across the street. I'd gotten so used to being tall here; he towers over me and I feel powerless, like a child.

We circle the museum to the back door. "I know you have a key," he says.

I don't bother pretending like I don't. I'm too busy trying to figure out what he wants. I'd dismissed him as a slimy lech, but I'd underestimated the cunning beneath his jackal face.

I open the door, and we walk through the now empty museum. A security guard, the one with the goatee and kind eyes, looks up from his chair by the stairs. I smile; it feels like a death mask, but does the job as I see the tension leave his shoulders.

"Forgot my purse."

He waves us by and then we are in the pitch-black room, my room, where only a few minutes ago Ry broke my heart.

I laugh, a desperate, choking noise.

"What's funny?" Anubis snaps, looking for a light switch.

"Guess I should have let him read his stupid poem." Because whatever else the Greek liar is, he never made my soul clench with cold, salt-dried terror the way Anubis is. I can feel the tendrils of darkness seeping off him, clutching at me.

"Where are the lights?" he growls. His jaw snaps as he bites off the end of the sentence.

I lean down and flick them on. "You can't take any of it. Touch anything, and an alarm will go off." I'd briefly considered setting off an alarm myself, but I don't want the security guard to get hurt. He doesn't deserve it.

It's obvious now that Anubis has been after something in this room the whole time. The break-in at Sirus's house, the attack on the driver, the eyes I felt watching me—he was waiting for his chance to access my mother's artifacts. I have no idea why. He's been in our Abydos home countless times, and junk like this is all over the place.

"I don't need to take it." He drags me over to the largest fresco, the one of my mother and Horus with the sun god. And then he stares at it, searches it like he would devour it with his eyes.

"What are you looking for?" I try to see what he's seeing.

A low growl sounds at the back of his throat, and his hand tightens on my skin, now stinging and cracked with dryness.

I don't ask anything else.

Why *this* fresco? Why leave his base of power in Egypt to stare at this one dumb painting that tells a story everyone knows? I look from the image of my mother, to falcon-headed Horus, to prone Amun-Re. There's nothing there!

Then I notice Anubis's lips are moving ever so slightly, as though he's trying to read. I'm looking at the wrong part of the picture. The glyphs that surround the figures—the ones only I can read, because only I know how to translate my mother's writing.

This is the story of my mother learning the most powerful god's name, written by Isis herself. Chaos. He's here to figure out Amun-Re's true name. And if someone like Anubis could control the sun god . . .

"Here," he says, jabbing his finger at the beginning of the writing. "Read it."

"I can't."

"Don't try to lie to me. You can live a long time with

just your heart and lungs working, but it will hurt very, very much." He leans in so close I can feel his breath leeching the moisture from my skin. I am actually cracking under his gaze. "You can read your mother's writing. Read it."

I don't want to die. Not here, not like this. Not in a way that will leave my soul without a path back to my father.

Oh, Dad. I'm sorry.

I look up at the fresco. "It's . . . it's just the story. You already know it."

"Read every word."

Trembling, I start at the beginning. "Isis protected Horus, keeping him safe from the wrath of Set. But cunning Isis knew that hiding Horus would not be enough. She wanted the true name of Amun-Re, god of the sun, god of the gods. Only by wielding it together would Horus be ready to challenge Set for Egypt. She lured Amun-Re from the sky, where a child of—I don't know this word."

"Sound it out," he says, gripping my arm so hard that I've lost all feeling in my hand.

"Ah-pep. Where a child of Ah-pep waited to bite him. Amun-Re, poisoned and dying, implored Isis to use her magic and save him. She would not until he had given his true name to her son."

"Where is that? Where are you reading?"

I point to the section of text. He narrows his eyes, then leans back, a satisfied sneer curling his thin lips. "That's all I needed."

"What do you need that for? You know that story! Amun-Re, the snake, the name." I stare, desperate, at what I've just read. He must see something I don't, something hidden in my mother's words.

He spins me around and marches me out of the room. I wish prayer worked, because I don't have even that hope now.

"My stuff. You ripped up my stuff. And you took Sirus's scrapbook."

"I didn't anticipate them valuing Isis's things so highly. Imagine my disappointment when it wasn't stored at your brother's home. I'd hoped at the very least you had a key for your mother's inane scrawlings, but no. I've had to wait all this time."

He squeezes my arm as we leave the room. "I like you. You see what an insufferable worm your mother is. And you've finally given me what I've needed all these aching ages." He nods pleasantly at the security guard and I stumble numbly beside him as we leave the museum.

He takes me down the stairs and into the canyon. It's dark, darker than it should be, low clouds blotting out the stars that used to watch over me.

I *refuse* to die under a cloudy sky. I pretend to trip, throwing myself into a sprawling heap on the ground. Anubis's hand on my arm nearly rips it from its socket, and my shoulder smashes painfully into the dirt as a sharp rock cuts my knee.

Anubis growls, his vocal cords shifting from human to something more raw, lower.

"Sorry," I whimper, closing my hands over the rock as I push myself back up. I stand, and before he can fix his grip, I smash the rock into the side of his head and run as fast as I can for the beginning of the canyon and the stairs.

I'm almost there when hands push me from behind. My own momentum propels me forward, the asphalt at the bottom of the stairs shredding my palms before my head slams into and bounces off the lowest step. Lights explode in my vision and I can't see past the pain bouncing around my skull.

"Did you think you could get away from me, you stupid, mortal child?" His voice is a tortured nightmare imitation of a person. "I am a *god*."

"Only in Egypt," Ry says, and my vision clears in time to see Anubis look up, his face twisted in rage, just as a fist smashes into his jaw. He reels backward, snarling, then a hissing noise cuts through the night, and my eyes and nose burn.

Anubis's scream turns into a high-pitched, desperate animal whine as he paws at his eyes, spinning in circles.

"Come on!" Tyler says, pulling me up. My head swims and I trip on the stairs. Ry's arm is immediately around me, and the three of us run from dry, crackling, salty death, still howling in the canyon behind us.

Amun-Re sits at the head of the pantheon of gods. He is without beginning or end, having created himself out of the nothing. He is the god of the sun, the god of creation, so powerful that he is King of the Gods. His names are endless, his titles infinite, but only one name is secret. Only one name allows those who know it to claim a position next to his throne.

Only one name allows those who know it to appeal directly to his power, to use it for themselves. For whatever end.

"YOU SHOULD GO TO THE HOSPITAL," TYLER says, her voice high and rushed with adrenaline as she bounces against the door of Ry's truck. I'm smashed in the middle between the two of them.

"I'm fine." It's a lie. I am not fine. My head is a symphony of pain, a sadistic master maestro conducting an opus of excruciating, devastating perfection. I can't remember how we got into the truck, or how long we've been driving. Ry's dashboard is slowly rising and falling like it's on ocean waves instead of street asphalt.

The bright side is that I barely feel my palms, though

in the occasional illumination of the streetlights we pass they look like they had a run-in with a cheese grater. Also I keep seeing other lights that aren't actually there.

"We should call nine-one-one," she says.

"Wait, that's a real number?" I ask.

"What do you mean?"

"I thought it was a movie number. Like how they always use five-five-five for phone numbers. So that people wouldn't accidentally use the real number for calling the police."

Tyler chokes out a laugh. "No, it's real. And I'm not sure why we haven't called it yet. We should report that guy!"

"Can't arrest a god."

Ry coughs sharply. "You're confused."

"Seriously!" Tyler leans forward to try and look at my eyes. I swat her away. "He was going to hurt you! He did hurt you! I really think you have a concussion."

He was going to do something much worse than hurt me. He *is* going to do something much worse than hurt me. "Police can't help. He's probably already gone. And he *is* my half brother."

"Seriously?"

"Seriously." I don't have my phone and I don't have any numbers memorized. I have to get home so I can call my mother. Warn her. My stomach turns and threatens to rebel, and it isn't only because of the pain and nausea I'm

241

swimming in. If Anubis did figure it out—if, all the many gods forbid, he learned the true name of the sun god from that fresco . . . The thought of Anubis with that much power makes me want to vomit. But I'm alive. I can still fix this.

"Thank you, guys. If you hadn't come . . . well, thank you."

Tyler has my wrist in her hand. "Isadora, you already said that. Four times. We need to go to the hospital."

"No! I need to get home and call my parents. How did you know to come help me?"

Her voice is patient, the same tone she uses in the Children's Discovery Room. "Like I already explained, *three times*, girl-who-does-not-have-a-concussion, as soon as I realized he was the guy who was asking about you earlier, I knew something was up. I'm so glad my mom made me swear to always carry pepper spray. And that I found Ry."

Ry, who I threatened to kill earlier tonight, and who still didn't hesitate to help me when I needed it most. Ry, who is not who he was. Ry, whose betrayal somehow stings far deeper than Anubis's, and I don't know why it hurts so much. It shouldn't hurt so much. But he's like my parents—building a foundation and then ripping it away, changing the rules.

Oooh, I hate him and I hate this truck and I hate the hills of San Diego and the way they make me want to lean over and throw up in dear Tyler's lap. I need to be home. Now. I need to warn my mother.

Tyler's phone rings and she answers it, breathlessly spilling out her version of the story to Scott. When she hangs up, she tells Ry that Scott will pick her up at my house.

"I'm going to stay there tonight," Ry answers.

"Excuse me?" I hold the side of my head like I can contain the pain if I push hard enough.

"I'm not leaving you alone."

"First of all, you are not welcome at my house. Second of all, I have a brother and a sister-in-law there."

"You also have a concussion." Tyler pulls one of my hands away to try and see my eyes again. She keeps muttering something about pupils. "Also, where the crap did you get this amazing bracelet? Is it real gold?"

"I don't want to talk about it," I mumble. I want to rip it off, but I can't figure out how to undo the clasp. Another sneaky, underhanded move by Ry.

I hurt, everything hurts, and I am so hurt that he lied to me. That he always understood me even more than I thought he could, but he didn't *tell* me that he understood. I don't think he's evil, not now that Anubis revealed himself, but still.

Ry's the son of gods. It changes everything.

"No, seriously, that's real gold, isn't it? Maybe that's why your crazy half brother was after you! This has to be worth serious money."

243

"Yeah, maybe." Gold is not really a commodity at my house. The name of the sun god, however . . .

Ry pulls to a stop in front of Sirus's house. Scott's car is already parked there and Tyler jumps out of the truck and runs to him, throwing her arms around his neck. My stone heart thumps forlornly in my chest as I watch them, and my traitor body longs for the comfort of another person.

I get out of the truck instead, and limp and stagger toward the dark house. *This must be what it feels like to be drunk,* I think, as the ground bucks and rolls around me.

"It doesn't look like anyone's home."

I startle, so lost in my pain and my determination to call my mother that I didn't notice Ry get out after me. "They're probably in bed."

"I'll wait until you know for sure that they're home and you've told Sirus what happened. I'm assuming that was Anubis. What did he really want?"

"It's a family matter." My teeth are clenched so hard my jaw aches and I can feel my pulse as a stabbing pain in my forehead. "Go home."

"Sure you're okay?" Tyler calls out from the curb. I wave dismissively. "Call me first thing in the morning, then. And I just Googled concussions. Don't take ibuprofen, take Tylenol."

Scott opens her door. "And next time you get in a fight, do it when I'm around. I'm good at the punching!"

I'm too tired to respond. I open the door; the entire house is dark. Sirus is a night owl. He should still be up. Maybe something *is* wrong here, too. Panicked that Anubis got to them, I take a deep breath.

It smells like Tide. I collapse against the doorframe in relief. Anubis hasn't been here.

Ry steps forward like he's going to come in with me.

"Please," I say. It hurts to talk. "Thank you for tonight. Really. You saved my life. But I can't—I can't handle you right now. I'm confused, and I don't know how this changes things, but it does. And until I know how it changes things, I just—I need you to be somewhere else."

He swallows, then nods. I shut the door behind myself. I want him far away. I want him right here. I don't know how I want him. But my mother. I need to talk to my mom.

Flipping lights on as I go, I find a note on the table. Sirus's hasty scrawl is nearly illegible.

> *Isadora—tried your cell, Deena sick, going to the hospital, call me.*
> *—S*

No! I grab the phone and dial Sirus's cell. It takes me three tries to get the numbers right, then it goes straight to voice mail, so I tell him to please call on this line because my cell is gone. My fluttery, panicked feeling intensifies. I don't want anything to happen to Deena, or to their baby.

They need to be okay. I need them to be okay, and to be a dorky, happy couple and raise a dorky, happy kid.

Please let her be okay.

My mother, fortunately, picks up on the second ring. "Who is this?" She sounds exhausted. I don't remember the time difference, if it's the middle of the night there or what.

"It's Isadora."

"What happened? Are you okay? You're hurt!"

My voice catches. "I'm okay. But something bad happened. Anubis was here."

"What? Why would he be there?"

I relay the story to her—all of it, including the driver who was attacked and the times I felt like I was being watched, and some of the details are out of order because I can't quite organize my thoughts like I know I should be able to, but eventually I tell her everything. "Mom, I had to read it for him. I'm so sorry. I think—I think he figured out Amun-Re's real name." I hold my breath, waiting for her reaction. How bad is it going to be? How much power did I help that jackal-faced monstrosity get?

Then my mother laughs. It's a tired, worn-out laugh, more air than mirth. "Oh, Little Heart. You don't need to worry about this."

"He can control the sun god now!"

"No, he can't. He may have thought he found something there, but I can assure you that Amun-Re's true name isn't recorded anywhere. Surely you don't think I'd go to all that trouble to get it for myself and Horus and then write it down where any slovenly god of embalming could find it?"

I slump onto a chair, relieved and confused. "Then what did he find? Because he seemed happy."

"Anubis is a fool, and like all fools will easily believe what he wants to believe. He probably found something in the text he thought was Amun-Re's true name. He'll come back and try to use it, and then he'll be sent scurrying with his tail between his legs. And I assure you that after I have this baby, he will have a serious reckoning to face for threatening you."

"So you're safe," I say, and for the first time since I kissed Ry—oh no I kissed Ry and then he told me the truth, and it's like I'm remembering it for the first time all over again what is wrong with my brain—the steel bands around my lungs release.

"I am safe. And I'm glad you are, too. How did you get away from Anubis?"

"Some friends helped me out."

"I'm so glad you made good friends."

I think of Ry, his parents, the truth. I should tell her who—what—he is. She should know there are other gods out there. But if I told her, I have no doubt I'd never see Ry again.

I should want that.

"I'm glad, too," I say instead. "Okay. Yay, it isn't the end of the world." My hands sting like crazy holding the phone, and I want to sink into the couch and sleepy oblivion. "I'm gonna go take something for my head. I'll call you tomorrow."

"I'll look forward to it. Oh, and Isadora?"

"Yeah?"

"I'll want to hear all about how the gala went before your bastard half brother showed up."

"Okay." I smile. She remembered. "Good night."

"Good night, Little Heart."

I hang up, and now that my initial relief is past, I am back to worrying about Deena. After I wash my hands and pick the tiny bits of gravel out of them, I change out of my ruined dress into pajamas and bandage my various scrapes. I can't get the stupid bracelet off. I'll make Ry take it off me tomorrow.

There's some p.m. painkiller combo in the cupboard—did Tyler say ibuprofen was bad or good? I can't remember. I don't care. The phone rings, and I stare at it for a few seconds before realizing I have to answer.

"What?"

"Hey, kiddo."

"Sirus! What's going on? What happened to Deena? Is she okay? Is the baby okay?"

"They're both okay. Sorry if the note scared you. It was kind of a scary night." He laughs drily, and I couldn't agree more, though this is definitely not the time to tell him about my mini family reunion. "After we left the museum Deena was really dizzy and her stomach hurt. We went straight to the hospital, and she's fine now, on bed rest until they decide whether she needs to deliver the baby sooner rather than later."

"But she's not due yet!"

"She's far enough along that it might be safer for both of them to get him here." He swears softly. "Oh, thank goodness, she's asleep. She didn't hear me call him a him. Anyway. It's something called preeclampsia, and since we know it's an issue one way or another, we'll deal with it and keep both of them perfectly healthy. But we aren't going to be home for a while, probably. Are you okay? Do you need anything?"

"I'm fine! Don't worry about me. But I don't understand how this happened. Deena was totally healthy a few days ago." Had Anubis done something to her?

"It's just one of those things. Pregnancy leaves women vulnerable in a lot of ways. But I mean it—you don't need to worry. The only problem we're facing now is a baby without a nursery, which in the grand scheme of things isn't such a big deal."

I sigh, relieved. At least one part of my family is safe from Anubis. "Great. Thanks for the guilt, there, Sirus."

After again reassuring me that everything is fine, he hangs up.

I sink into the couch, not bothering to go upstairs, and my aching head spins with everything that happened tonight. It's too much to process. Deena, Anubis, Ry. I thought everything would be *easier* after I finished the stupid museum room.

I snort a sleepy giggle as I think of Anubis's face when he gets back to Egypt and realizes he doesn't have the name. What an idiot.

Happy with that thought, I'm on the very edge of sleep when I remember Sirus's words, similar to what my mother had said: a woman is most vulnerable when she's pregnant. Something tickles at the back of my numbed skull, something I'm not quite grasping but know I need to.

"Oh, no." I sit straight up, terrified in the certainty of my new realization.

Anubis wasn't looking for a name to control a god.

He was looking for a poison to kill one.

One day as Amun-Re walked the earth, a snake bit him. But it was no snake he had created, and so he could not name it and remove the poison. Amun-Re, god of the sun, was dying.

A snake. The myths only ever said a snake. But a version written in Isis's own hand had one key difference—not a snake, but a child of Apep. The snake demon found in the underworld.

The underworld only Osiris and Anubis could freely visit.

"PICK UP!" I SCREAM INTO THE PHONE AS IT rings and rings and rings. Screaming makes my head throb, but I can't stop. I stumble upstairs, throwing everything out of my drawers as I look for my passport. My hand closes over the small bag of protective amulets my mother sent, the ones that survived Anubis's destruction of my room. I shove them into the pocket of my flannel pajama pants.

Passport passport where is my passport ANSWER THE PHONE MOTHER ANSWER IT ANSWER IT.

Passport in the nightstand.

She's not answering the phone.

I pull on a pair of shoes and run down the stairs, this time calling Sirus.

He doesn't answer, either.

Email she'll check her email. I write one so fast I'm sure it's incoherent but it doesn't matter because she needs to know. I have to know that she knows.

Still the phone cradled against my ear rings and rings and rings. Why isn't she answering the phone? He can't be there yet. He still has to fly back to Egypt. Where I need to be, where I should be. The images, so many of them, of my mother being unmade by darkness play on repeat in my pounding head and I can't let that happen, I won't let that happen.

Why would Anubis do this? What does he stand to gain by killing my mother? What did he say to me . . . something about Hathor saying I was useless. The hall. They were kissing in the hall.

Hathor. If anyone has a reason to hate my mother and want her dead, it's Hathor. She must have seduced Anubis and gotten him to work for her. How long has she been planning this, plotting to strike when my mother is most vulnerable?

"ANSWER!" I scream into the phone, then throw it against the wall.

Airport. I'll go to the airport and get on the next flight to Egypt. It's a stupid plan, some part of me knows that, but I can't sit here. Either my mom will check her email or she won't, but I can't sit here and wait and wait to see whether or not I'll have a mother to go home to.

How to get to the airport, though? I laugh bitterly at the irony of staying with a brother who arranges transportation to the airport for a living but having no idea how to do it for myself. Screw it, I'll drive. I grab the keys to the Mini off the counter and run into the garage, opening it.

The key fits in the ignition, then nothing happens. I put the key in. WHY IS NOTHING HAPPENING? I twist it, and the radio and lights come on, but the engine is still off. "Start! Start! *Why won't you start?*" I sob, smashing my bloodied palms against the steering wheel.

Even if I get the car started, I literally have no idea how to drive it or how to get to the airport from here. My forehead drops against the steering wheel and I cry because I am powerless and I've always been powerless and I hate, hate, hate it. How can I have a happy heart and helping hands when I can't help the woman who spent her whole life helping me, the woman I spent the last three years hating?

A hand comes down softly on my shoulder and I scream, sitting up straight.

"It's me! Sorry. I didn't mean to scare you." Ry holds out a hand to help me out of the car.

I stare at him. "What are you still doing here?"

"I said I wasn't going to leave until you told me that

Sirus was here and everything was okay. I meant it. I've been sitting in my truck researching concussions."

I take his hand and almost fall getting out of the car. "I need to get to the airport. I have to go to Egypt right now."

"Why?"

"Because they're going to kill my mom! Hathor and Anubis are going to kill her, and she's not answering her phone, and if she dies there will be no one strong enough to bring her back to life."

"Come on," he says, grabbing my hand and running with me to his truck. He peels out, dialing his phone. "Mom, we need the Lear. Isadora's family is in trouble."

"I don't know how to buy a plane ticket," I say, desperation and despair washing over me.

Ry looks at me, the phone still to his ear. "You don't need to. We're going to fly you to Egypt. My family has a plane; it's gassed up and ready for a trip my parents were going to take tomorrow."

"But—"

"It will take a fraction of the time flying a normal plane would. I'm going to get you there, and we're going to save your mom. I promise."

He goes back to the conversation and nods. "Okay, yeah, tell Aunt Iris we need her there now. Thanks, Mom. I love you." He hangs up, then hands me the phone. "Keep trying your mom."

"Thank you." My voice cracks. "Thank you." I dial the

number I now have memorized, then listen, each ring sounding longer and farther away. It rings and rings and rings.

A bump jars me awake. I don't know where I am or why the whole world is dim and shaking. There are leather seats that look like armchairs, and wood paneling, but it's narrow and . . .

My mother. The jet. Ry. I rub my eyes, my stomach roiling with motion sickness. The combination of concussion (I will never admit to Tyler that I actually have one) and the sleep-aid pain meds I took has left me utterly disoriented. Ry tried valiantly to keep me awake, but I dropped off several times.

"We're getting close," Ry says, opening the shade to look out the window. Another bunch of turbulence makes my teeth rattle.

"Is it always this bumpy?"

He runs a hand through his hair and smiles sheepishly. "Well, we're getting a little help. Iris, the pilot and my, uh, aunt? She's married to Zephyrus. He's kind of the west wind. So he's been speeding us along."

I can't get past how weird it is that he has the same type of family I do. He must have as many crazy stories as as me. I think I'd like to hear them someday.

"Did my mother call?"

"No. I've tried calling her every fifteen minutes. No answer."

255

I nod, pursing my lips and gritting my teeth.

"Do you have a plan?"

"Get home. Warn my mother. That's about the extent of it."

"And if Anubis and Hathor are there?"

I finger the amulets in my pocket, rubbing their contours like I can will the magic toward my mother. "I'll figure something out."

He looks like he wants to say something else, then he nods. "Okay."

I wish I were still asleep. Sitting here in the air, doing nothing while my mother could be dying right now, could already be dead . . . "Can we go any faster?"

"Not without risking the whole jet falling apart."

I grab fistfuls of my hair and pull, so frustrated and scared I feel like I am fraying apart at the edges.

"I'm sorry." His voice is so utterly sincere that another piece of my stone heart flakes off, stabbing into my ribs. I was stupid to think he'd hurt me or my family. Whatever else I know or don't know about him, I know that at least.

"Don't be sorry. You've already helped me so much. I'd probably still be on a layover somewhere, if I'd even figured out how to get to the airport. You . . . you were there for me. Again. Thank you." I stare at the ceiling to avoid his eyes.

"I will always be here to help you however I can." There's a long pause. "Since I have you pretty much captive,

I want to explain some things. I know it's a bad time, but it might be my only time, and I need you to understand."

I slump lower into the leather chair, more an armchair than an airplane seat. "I can't do this right now."

"You don't have to do anything. Just listen. You don't have to respond, or answer. I'm sorry that I didn't tell you about my parents. I promise that everything else was true and real, and I'm only seventeen and not a god and never will be. I should have told you sooner, and I should have realized that it might not be a happy revelation for you. When I figured out you were the same as me, it made everything feel even more right, but it was stupid and selfish of me to assume you'd feel the same way about it. Oh! I forgot." He gets up and, holding on to seats and the wall to stay steady in the wildly bumpy air, opens a small fridge and pulls out a Coke.

"Bribery?" I take it anyway, desperately needing sugar and caffeine. My mother was right—it is *so* addicting. Of course she was right. Oh, Mom. Be okay.

"You know, the poem said all of this a lot better. I even betrayed Calliope and went with Erato as my muse so I could make it lyric poetry instead of epic. Calliope was pissed, too. Um. So." His long, olive fingers pick nervously at the dress pants he's still wearing from last night. "I guess we're kind of opposites, because you've spent the last few years determined to love no one, and I've spent the last few years determined to find you."

I want to yell at him, to tell him dreams are a perfectly awful way to make life decisions, until I remember my strange obsession with Orion. Not the one next to me, but the stars, and the way they made me feel safe and loved when I didn't have anything else. The way that feeling seemed to jump to Ry against my will.

"It's stupid to fall in love with someone because of dreams," I finally say.

"But that's just it! I didn't fall in love with you because of the dreams. All the dreams told me was that you were out there, somewhere. They made me look for you. And then I found you, and I didn't fall in love with you."

What the crap? I raise an eyebrow at him, and he grins.

"I didn't *fall* in love with you. I walked into love with you, with my eyes wide open, choosing to take every step along the way. I do believe in fate and destiny, but I also believe we are only fated to do the things that we'd choose anyway. And I'd choose you; in a hundred lifetimes, in a hundred worlds, in any version of reality, I'd find you and I'd choose you."

I can't look at his eyes, because they are too blue, too sincere, with too much flooding in, and I cannot swim. "I don't know. I can't—you don't even know me; you shouldn't love me. I'm mean and I'm cold and I don't know if I even can love someone else yet, or if I want to, and—"

"Isadora." The floods and crashing waves quiet. "You are not mean or cold. You're strong and funny and smart and beautiful. And okay, maybe sometimes you are a little bit mean, but like you said, it's a fine line between confident and arrogant, and someone has to help me walk it, right? I've found my path, and I'm going to stay on it. I wanted you to know how I feel, and also to know that it's okay to feel however you feel because I'm a very, very patient person."

"What if I decide my *destiny* is someone else?"

"Then that's your decision and I would respect that. Also I know a whole lot of gods to smite whoever it is you choose instead of me."

"You—"

"Kidding! Totally kidding. Mostly kidding. Okay, not really kidding."

I laugh, and it hurts my head but it frees a little bit of the pain in my chest. "Can we finish talking about this after I save my mother?"

"Absolutely." He leans back, smiling and obviously relieved. "That went better than I thought. You didn't yell at me. But for the record, the poem had some really amazing imagery with the desert and the ocean and flowers waiting to bloom."

"That probably would have gotten you yelled at."

"Prepare for landing," a cheery voice crackles over the intercom. "There's no runway here, so it might be rough."

Not as rough as what I'll face after we land. I buckle my seat belt and start praying to every god I can think of that my mother is still okay.

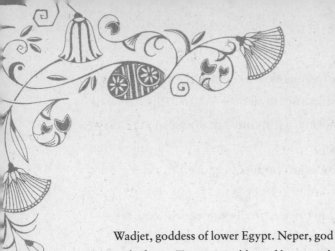

Wadjet, goddess of lower Egypt. Neper, god of grain. Montu, god of war. Taweret, goddess of home and childbirth. Baba, god of aggression and virility. Khonsu, god of the moon. Tayet, goddess of weaving. Sia, god of divine knowledge. Shay, god of destiny.

These are gods who were prayed to, worshipped, feared. Gods who had altars and temples, gods who had priesthoods, gods whose names were whispered and revered and remembered.

Nothing is truly eternal. No one remembers them now.

Do they have an afterlife?

I SPRINT THROUGH THE OPEN DESERT, CLOUDS of dust the jet kicked up billowing behind me. The arid wind clears my sinuses, clears my fuzzy head, fills and focuses me. Ry runs, too, but I'm faster than him and I don't wait. I can't.

I make it to the stone steps that lead down to my house, then curse. Ry won't be able to see them. I turn back but he's still a hundred yards away, his uneven gait slowing him.

Floods! I rip off my long-sleeved pajama shirt, glad I

wore a sports bra, and leave the shirt half in and half out of the entryway. Maybe the half that mysteriously disappears will clue Ry in to my mother's magical barrier. It's the best I can do.

I trip down the stone steps and burst through the front door into my empty, empty family room. "Mom!" I scream. "Mom! Dad!" I run through the room, down the hall into the old stone section toward her bedroom.

Someone steps out of the supply room into the hall and I slam into them, falling back. "Nephthys?" If she's here, my mom's probably still okay! I made it in time!

She looks shocked to see me. "Child! What are you doing here?"

"My mom's in trouble! Anubis and Hathor are going to try to kill her!"

Her face, so like my mother's—but softer, like she's always a bit out of focus—goes white. "Oh, no."

"Where is she? We need to tell her."

"Hathor—I didn't know—she went down into the tombs. With Isis."

"No!" I turn back to the other end of the hall, to the door I spent so many years avoiding. The stairs seem to stretch into infinity, into the very bowels of the earth, and I nearly throw myself down them to go faster. The tombs and paintings are a blur as I run, shouting my mother's name.

Finally, breathless with terror and surrounded only by the silent dead, I burst through into the main chamber, my father's throne room. His chair is there, with statue-still Ammit in front of it.

Otherwise it's totally empty.

"MOM!" I scream. I must have missed them. The tombs—one of the tombs—there are so many. I spin around to see Nephthys behind me in the entry.

"I didn't see them! Did you?"

She cocks her head to the side, her black eyes calm, collected, clearer than I've ever seen them. It hits me that, in all my life, I've never seen her keep eye contact until now.

"What am I going to do with you?" she asks.

I move to run back into the hall, but she blocks me. I shake my head, desperate. She doesn't understand how little time we have. "What are you—oh." My whole body wilts, mirroring my soul. "Not Hathor," I whisper.

She taps her chin thoughtfully, her eyes never leaving me.

"Why?" My voice is strangled, choked by my failure to figure it out the right way. My failure to protect my mother like she would have protected me.

"You have such spirit, such determination to create your own self free of Isis. Everyone should have that. I should have that. I've spent millennia atoning for the sin of wanting more than I was given, more than a powerless, contemptible husband who never loved me, who wouldn't even stoop to giving me a child. Wanting more for my son, who has as much birthright as Isis's. We are all forgotten gods, but I *will* claim what should always have been mine. Chaos created an opening after all this time, and I will end my sister and take her place. I will become Isis."

"She loves you!"

"Don't be naive. Isis loves nothing but her own greatness. This whole world is merely her mirror, and if it doesn't reflect back her own distorted view of her magnificence, she breaks it until it does."

I stand straighter. "She loves me."

My aunt waves dismissively. "You are a toy. And I am done here."

"I don't understand!" I have to keep her here, talking. If my mother were already dead, Nephthys wouldn't have sent me down here. There's still time. "Why did you need Anubis?"

She finally looks away, down the corridor behind her at something I can't see. "Cursing Isis with everything I had wasn't enough." All those times Mom sounded so tired—and talked about how Nephthys was helping her. I feel sick. It should have been me here. I would have helped. I would have known.

That's not true. I wouldn't have cared enough to see. But now I do.

Nephthys nods toward me, still looking at something else. "We needed the *exact* venom to kill a god, which Isis had very kindly recorded. Not just any snake. Apep."

"You can't," I whisper, beg.

"I can." She looks back at me and smiles, but her smile has none of the warmth my mom's has. "Good-bye, child."

She turns, and I jump forward to tackle her but another body, lean with cruel sinew and reeking of desiccation, blocks me.

"Your mother is about to deliver her very last mewling whelp," Anubis says. "And then my mother will deliver them both to the underworld."

I scream and claw at his face, gouging long trails of crimson before he throws me to the ground. He says a word I don't know, and it echoes through me and around the room like the sharp crack of thunder from dry heat lightning.

Something moves behind me.

"Meet the lovely demon Ammit." His teeth cut a vicious smile. "She doesn't much care for this world, but I've woken her especially for you. Now I've got some tombs to prepare."

I stand, trembling, too scared to turn around. With a snarling laugh Anubis walks away, calling over his shoulder, "Try not to upset her stomach."

I slowly spin to find myself staring at each of Ammit's sharp, yellowed crocodile teeth, her mouth a gaping black void. Her breath washes over me, and it smells like blood and judgment and death.

Ammit snaps her long, scaled, gray-green mouth shut, turning her head to the side and fixing one huge slit-pupiled yellow eye on my chest directly over my heart. I wish I were wearing a shirt. I wish I were wearing armor.

"Don't eat it don't eat it don't eat it." I shut my eyes and think of all the times I played around her legs as a child, the picnics I had with my back resting against her strong hippo feet, the desert flowers I'd bring to decorate her with. Shouldn't she know me?

A voice as old and as hungry as time rings through my head. *That is no longer your heart. I devour untrue hearts.*

I squeeze my closed eyes so tightly it hurts. My heart is stone. My heart is the desert. My heart is a horizon stretching on forever, sand and sky and empty beautiful perfection.

An untrue heart, she declares, and I feel the warm, sticky breath of death and I never wanted to die and it will hurt and without my heart I can't be complete in the underworld no matter what my dad does. There will be no afterlife for me.

"Isadora!" Ry's voice bounces off the walls, and my heart leaps because he called my name. He's here, and he won't find this room in the labyrinth of tombs so he'll be safe, and he can help my mother after I'm dead. I'm flush with relief and holding on to my name as Orion says it, holding on to the bright, steady hope my stars-made-human fills me with.

There is your truth. Her laughter—part lion's growl, part hippo's bellow, part crocodile's hiss—tumbles through my head. I open my eyes, shocked, and she sits down on her hippo haunches.

"You aren't going to eat me?"

She yawns, and a new view of the teeth that nearly ripped away both my life and afterlife sends me scurrying out of the room and right into Ry's arms.

"Isadora! In there?" He looks toward the throne room.

"NO! She'll eat your—" I pause, then roll my eyes. "You'd probably be fine. My mom's not here. Back upstairs!"

I run down the winding corridor and take the stairs three at a time. "Watch out for Anubis and Nephthys!"

"I thought Hathor." He gasps from behind me as we come out to the main hallway.

"No! Just—black hair, not pregnant, secretly evil."

"Got it!"

A growl sounds from the stairs behind. I turn to see Anubis charging up the steps after us. He must have been in one of the side tombs. Ry slams the door shut and braces himself against it, jamming one of his legs against the wall at an angle.

"Go! I've got this!"

"Don't let him touch you! Run if he gets out!" My feet pound on the rug and I slam my shoulder into my mom's heavy wooden door, exploding into her bedroom.

I take it all in with a glance. My father, calmly at my

mother's bedside, holding her hand. My mother, in bed, her raised knees contoured under a white sheet, her face sweaty and flushed. And Nephthys, bending over a covered woven basket in the corner.

Our eyes meet. Hers flash with the malice of millennia. She snatches the basket and rips off the lid, jerking the basket toward my mom and flinging the long golden demon snake through the air.

"No!" I scream, launching myself in front of the bed, hands raised.

The snake, coiled body twisting and fangs wide, comes down.

On my wrist.

Here's the thing about the ancient Egyptians: they were smart. They had a lot of things figured out ages before anyone around them. They built monuments that still stand, that still elicit wonder from all who behold them. Their art continues to fascinate generations later. Their religion was complex and evolved with them.

But sometimes they were so caught up in the business of studying and preparing for the afterlife, they failed to live. Death loomed so heavily in their minds that they stopped being able to see anything but this final mystery, this final aspect of life they couldn't understand, couldn't control.

The fear of death can grow so large we let it keep us from living.

Birth and rebirth.

Chaos and order.

Life and death.

Balance.

TIME SLIPS FROM ITS STEADY, ETERNAL STREAM, slowing down like the whoosh, whoosh, whoosh of my heart.

A snake so venomous it can kill a god has its jaws

wrapped around my wrist. Why doesn't it hurt? It really should hurt.

Which is when I realize that its fangs aren't piercing my skin—one fang is jammed into the jade scarab beetle on my bracelet, stuck there, the broad gold of the bracelet keeping the free fang from my skin. I'm not going to die! I'm not going to die!

The snake writhes, its coiled and scaled body whipping through the air as it tries to free its fang.

"Isadora!" my mother screams. Oh, right. Get the snake *off* the wrist. I shake my arm wildly around, and the snake loses its grip, sailing through the air and landing with a thud on the floor at the foot of the bed.

It rises, hissing, mouth open impossibly wide. It seems to grow even as I watch, uncoiling and stretching until I'm sure it will grow past the entire room and swallow us all. I have no way to fight this, no way to protect my mother. I reach out my hand and it finds hers.

My father slams his staff onto the snake's tail. It freezes, drying into dust before my eyes, and then it's gone.

Nephthys sinks to her knees, eyes glued to the place where the demon snake no longer exists. "No," she whispers, trembling. "No." She doesn't look up, doesn't look at any of us.

Ry slides in, glancing over his shoulder. "Anubis is out! I couldn't hold the door anymore so I ran."

He turns to see the state of the room. Nephthys

cowering in the corner. My father with his black skin and mummy wrappings, standing impossibly tall, his staff rippling with power. And my mother in a decidedly awkward position on the bed.

"I'll just wait in the other corner, then." Ry sidles along the wall, staring at the floor.

"Isadora? Nephthys? What is going on?" Isis's voice is strained, her face beaded with sweat. She looks awful, dark shadows under her eyes, her skin sallow beneath its normally rich color. Maybe Nephthys did a better job with the curses than she thought.

There's a pendant around my mom's neck. "Did Nephthys make that for you?" I ask. She nods, and I pull it off and throw it across the room. Grabbing one of the true protection amulets from my pocket, I slip it over her head, then, hesitating, I lean over and brush a kiss across her forehead like she used to do for me when I didn't feel well.

She takes a deep breath, and her eyes sharpen as if the room has come back into focus, though her color is still way off. "Nephthys," she says, no anger in her voice as she looks at her sister sobbing quietly in the corner. "Dear sister. I am sorry."

"It was her," I say. "All along. The dreams—everything—it's always been her. She's the black poison that's been haunting us, threatening to destroy everything!"

"Little Heart." She smiles at me, and the sun blossoms in my chest. "Thank you. I am so glad you're here."

"What about her?" I glare at my aunt. "What are you going to do to her?"

"Nothing."

My jaw drops. "But—she—Mom, she tried to kill you! She tried to kill me, too!"

I tighten my fists. Nephthys deserves to die. No one as twisted and bitter as she is should have eternal life. It's a waste, and it's not fair.

For the briefest second I see black curling and pressing against the edge of my vision, but when I blink it's gone. My rage dies like a smothered fire. I won't feed that blackness. I wouldn't let it have my mother's soul; I won't let it have mine, either.

My mother sighs, and she sounds sad. "We will do nothing. We will forget her name."

"You can't," Nephthys says, crawling toward the bed. "You can't!"

My father shifts slightly, blocking her way forward. If any of this has ruffled his calm, I certainly can't tell. But something in his eyes when he looks at Nephthys tells me that in her grand plans she didn't account for what his wrath would have been if she had succeeded.

"I treasured your name," my mother says, looking at Nephthys and then deliberately looking away. "I wrote it on my heart. I will keep your name alive no longer."

Silently weeping, Nephthys stands and stumbles from the room. She seems smaller, dimmer, already diminished.

I wonder how long it will take her to fade now that she has lost my mother's love and magic. My rage spent, I feel sorry for her, sorry for the unfathomable spans of time she had and wasted.

I turn to my mother, smooth back a stray lock of hair from her forehead.

She smiles at me, lips dry and pulled tight over her teeth. "My brave, clever girl. As soon as I'm well, we'll go for a picnic on the Nile."

"I'd like that." I would. I'm ready to get to know her without the poison I let destroy our relationship, without the strain of misunderstanding between us. I'm actually excited about spending time together.

"And darling?"

"Yes?"

"What in the three kingdoms have you done to your hair? You're grounded."

Okay, new plan. Back to San Diego and getting to know her through the phone and email, instead.

"Oh! Osiris! It's time. Get the birthing stool." She smiles, then grimaces, and puts a hand over her stomach. Floods, *that* time. "Isadora, you've made this all possible. I would like you to deliver the baby."

And maybe what I said to Nephthys about my mother loving me isn't true after all, because that's just sick. "Mom, I'd take a demon snakebite for you, but I am so gone until that thing is out of your stomach and cleaned."

I turn toward the door. Ry's got his hands shoved in his pockets, broad shoulders pushed up. "Umm, vengeful goddess and crazed god of embalming out there?"

"Baby being squeezed out of my mother's birth canal in here."

He runs into the hall ahead of me. "Do you have any weapons?" he asks.

We both scream as we nearly plow into a man standing in the hall.

"Thoth?" I stare up into his small, kind eyes. "Please don't tell me you're secretly evil, too. I don't think I could handle it."

He smiles, turning both hands into birdies. "What's the problem?" one of them asks.

"Crazy Anubis and Nephthys tried to kill my mom. And me. They might still be around here."

The other hand-bird's eyes narrow murderously. It is way, *way* more threatening than I ever imagined a bird hand puppet could be. "I will take care of it," it croaks.

"Okay . . ."

Thoth's smile hasn't left, but he stands taller, and I notice a power about him that has always been disguised by his gentleness. "I have watched over your mother since before she was born. I will do the same for you, little one."

Beaming, I go on my tiptoes and kiss his wrinkled cheek. "I'm glad I always remembered you. And I promise I always will." Thoth nods, and I watch as his narrow, stooped frame disappears around the hall corner.

I doubt we'll see Anubis or Nephthys here again. I don't know how Set will feel about what his wife did, or about her decline. I don't know what it will mean if such a permanent part of their family disappears forever. But I am content to let my parents work out their own problems.

"Come on," I say, taking Ry's hand. "We can hide in my room."

Before locking the door behind us, I look in all the corners to double-check for lurking gods, but with Thoth here I feel calm. Safe.

"You have a bit of a theme," Ry says, looking around my room, which my mother hasn't destroyed yet. Thank goodness. I don't plan on staying here—what Sirus said about learning who we are away from our mother feels both true and timely. Now that I've finally accepted her and realized she always loved me, I think I can discover who I am without it revolving around what I'm not. San Diego seems like a good place to figure that out.

I flop onto the silver covers of my bed and stare at the ceiling. Ry jumps on next to me, bouncing me so hard I nearly fall off.

"Hey! There I am." He grins at the placement of Orion on my ceiling.

"I thought you said you weren't that Orion."

"Nope, just your Orion."

I roll my eyes, but I don't get up, and I don't move when

he casually scoots a bit closer to me. "Isadora?"

"Orion?"

"If we're going to go at a pace you want, it'd be really nice if you'd put a shirt on over your bra."

I sigh dramatically. "You're so demanding." But he has a point. In the rush to get away from the impending maternal nudity to end all maternal nudity, I'd kind of forgotten that I still hadn't replaced my shirt.

I stand and dig through my drawers for the clothes I have left here before settling on a plain black tee.

"You'll have to introduce me to your parents properly," Ry says. "You know, when you're not saving their lives. And when your mom's not in labor."

"Whatever you do, do *not* tell her you're Greek. She'll kick you out of the house and never let me see you again."

I turn around to find him staring at me, his blue eyes twin pools of happiness.

"So, you're seeing me?"

My fingers trace the jade oval of the scarab on my bracelet, the bracelet that saved more than one life today. A rebirth. Hope. "Maybe." I let a corner of my mouth go up in a smile. "For now. But don't think this means I buy any of your fate nonsense. I'm not committing to anything." Other than being happy and brave and willing to let temporary things feel permanent until maybe, just maybe, they *become* permanent.

He stands and wraps his arms around my waist, and

the shock and joy of his hands on me overwhelms my senses. I wonder if I'll ever get to the point where being touched doesn't do *this* to me. I hope not.

"Fortunately for us, I'm both persistent and persuasive." He leans in, and I smile against his lips, finally give up and let his love flood in and carve the last of my stone heart into a new shape I'm only just discovering.

Somehow it doesn't feel like a surrender.

It feels like a victory.

I wander the dark landscape, contentedly tracing the new constellations of my night sky. There, Isis, my mother—still infuriating but also beloved—and in her arms Dora, the first daughter named after someone other than herself. In the distance, farther than I can reach right now but in my future, my father's stars. Between us, Sirus and Deena's stars, even Tyler and Scott's. The stars and guiding points of my life, each in their place.

And of course, directly over me, Orion, with his new brilliantly blue stars. I reach up and trace my fingers along the milky swirls of the galaxy, decide where I'll paint my own stars onto the sky among these people I love.

Some things, the best things, do last forever.

FIRST THANKS, AS ALWAYS, TO NOAH (GOD OF making my whole life happy and having—you guessed it—amazing blue eyes), who is everything I know about love. Elena and Jonah (goddess and god of asking for snacks and being really adorable), thank you for being proud of what I do and usually helping me have enough time to do it.

This book would not have happened without Michelle Wolfson (goddess of delivering amazing news and gently shoving her clients in the right directions). It was her constant encouragement that gave me the guts to attempt this book again and again and again, even when I was ready to give up.

As always, huge thanks to my editor, Erica Sussman (goddess of obscenely cute dogs and much-appreciated exclamation marks). She never fails to take what I have *actually* written and show me how to turn it into what I *wanted* to have written.

Endless gratitude to Tyler Infinger (goddess of letting

me name characters I like after her) for assisting editorially and always being awesome, Christina Colangelo (goddess of fake karaoke) for being funny and delightful and super good at her job, Casey McIntyre (goddess of answering my stupid emails in a professional and friendly manner) for being a phenomenal publicist, Jessica Berg (goddess of fixing other people's mistakes) for being my stalwart copy editor, Kathryn Hinds (glorious goddess of abhorring alliteration) for helping my sentences make sense, Alison Donalty and Michelle Taormina (goddesses of creating beauty where nothing existed before) for continuing their streak of cover-art brilliance, and everyone else on the HarperTeen team (goddesses and gods of paper and words) for taking the art of making and selling books to such great heights.

Natalie Whipple (goddess of maintaining friends' sanity through daily chats), who always believed in Isadora and read every attempt at every draft of this book: you are amazing. Jon Skovron (god of indie bands you've never heard of but wish you were cool enough to know about) gave me excellent editorial advice when I was desperate for guidance before sending Isadora out into the world. Stephanie Perkins (goddess of baby sloths and adorability), who doesn't read every word I write, but helps me write all of them regardless.

Special thanks to Lorna Oakes and Lucia Gahlin, whose beautiful book *Ancient Egypt* was the foundation for my renewed interest in Egyptology as an adult.

Most especially, I am grateful to my parents, Pat and Cindy White. I wanted to write a book about that strange and terrifying space when you realize your parents aren't perfect. I'm so glad mine are imperfect in such perfect ways, and that they allowed their children to grow up as imperfect but perfectly loved people.

And finally, always, thanks to my readers: gods and goddesses of awesomeness and extremely good taste in fiction.

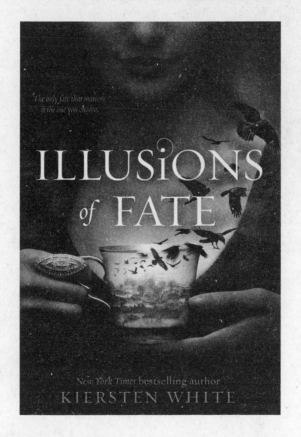

One

Dear Mama,

I am most certainly not dead. Thank you for your tender concern. I will try to write more often so you don't have to worry so between letters. (Because a week's silence surely means I have fallen prey to a wasting illness or been murdered in these boring, gray streets.)

School is going well. I am excelling in all of my classes. (Apparently, some things never change, and girls are not challenged in Albion in the same way they weren't on Melei.) My professors are *all intelligent and kind.* (Kind of horrible.) *None stand out.* (I refuse to mention *him* by name, no matter how many obviously "subtle" questions you ask.) *The other students are also quite focused on their schooling, and none of us has much time for socializing. Boys and girls attend separate classes as well, so no, I have not met many interesting young men.* (I am neither courting nor being courted. Please stop hoping.)

Tell Aunt Li'ne thank you for the mittens. They are very much appreciated in this cold, damp climate I am so unused to. And please tell the sun hello and I miss her very much! I also miss you, of course. (I do. Very much.)

All my love,

Jessamin

Reading over the letter to my mother, I am so absorbed in my head with adding the true statements to my written words that I fail to pay attention to the street. I cannot decide which shocks me more—nearly being run over by the horse-drawn cart, or the fluid stream of cursing in my native tongue that is being directed at me.

I look up, cheeks burning, and meet a pair of black eyes that, combined with the familiarity of the language, hit me with a longing for Melei so deep and painful I can scarcely draw a breath.

The man pauses, obviously surprised to see how dark of skin and eyes I am in spite of my school uniform. And so I take the opportunity to insult his manhood, his lineage, and his horse in a single, well-crafted turn of phrase I haven't used since my friend Kelen taught it to me when I was fourteen.

He smiles.

I smile back.

Brushing his hand through the air in another gesture so achingly familiar it brings tears to my eyes, he clicks his tongue and the cart moves on, our near-collision forgotten.

He's made me crave heat. The sun's anemic rays pull more warmth from me than they offer. I hate Albion, the whole gray country. I hate Avebury, a city just as gray, teeming with people but coldly lifeless.

No. Homesickness does me no good. Wiping under my eyes, I straighten my shoulders and march toward the hotel. I only have a couple of hours before my shift to do my reading for tomorrow's classes, and I will not be anything less than the best. I cannot afford it.

I cut away from the main thoroughfare and find myself in a narrow alley. It's old, the lines not quite vertical as they lean ever so gradually overhead.

"What's wrong, chickie bird?"

I startle, my eyes whipped down from where they traced the line of the sky. A man with the thick build, intricate tattoos, and accompanying ripe scent of a dockworker stands directly in front of me.

"Nothing." I flash a tight, dismissive smile honed these last few months of learning to blend in. "Just passing through."

"Nah, don't do that." He steps to the side as I do, and his mass blocks me from walking by. "Come have a drink with me, yeah? Make you feel all better."

"I have somewhere to be."

His smile broadens, blue eyes nearly lost in the tanned squint lines of his face. "You ain't from 'round here, are you? An island rat, that's what you are." He reaches out with a meaty hand to touch my hair, black as night and waterfall straight, where I have it pulled into a bun at the base of my neck.

"Excuse me." I back up but he follows, leaning in closer. "Let me by."

"I've heard stories about island rats. You can tell me if they're true."

I lift onto my toes to sprint away when a hand comes down on my shoulder.

"There you are, darling. So sorry I'm late."

I don't know this voice, a low tenor with the clipped, stylish vowels of the classes I only see when delivering orders to their expensive hotel rooms.

I stiffen under his fingers, which are light but steady on my shoulder. Now there are two of them to deal with. I slide my hand into my satchel, gripping the handle of the paring knife I borrowed from the kitchen and keep with me all the time. The gentleman's fingers tighten.

"Not necessary," he whispers.

I turn to look at him—a low, round hat is pulled over his forehead, obscuring his eyes. His lips are sly and twisted into a smile over teeth far finer than my dockworker friend's. This man is a porcelain doll compared to the brute blocking my path. He's taller than me but lean, all angles in his suit that reeks of money.

Apparently, the dockworker has the same assessment. "This your girl? I don't think she is."

"I would never accuse you of thinking, my good man." The gentleman lifts his silver-topped cane, tapping it once in the middle of the dockworker's forehead. "I shouldn't worry it'll be a problem for you to give up the practice of thinking entirely."

The dockworker blinks once—twice—so slowly I notice his stubby blond eyelashes, and then he moves to the side like he has forgotten how to walk on land.

"Good day, then." The gentleman steers me forward with his fingertips, and I've barely time to process what happened before we're out of the alley and back onto the main street.

"Well." I clear my throat, embarrassed. I look down the walkway instead of at the gentleman, not wanting to see in his eyes whether he did that out of the goodness of his heart or if he expects something in return. This is Albion, after all. "Thank you for your help. Good-bye."

"I'd like to walk you home, if it isn't too much trouble. Especially if you plan on gracing any more questionable streets with your presence."

I straighten my shoulders, sliding the right one out from

under his hand, and look him full in the face. His eyes are dark, his features fine, almost femininely delicate, save his strong jawline. "With all due respect, sir, I'm not about to trade one strange man for another, and I have no interest in showing you where I live."

His smile broadens. "Then I insist you let me buy you supper, and we will part as friends with no knowledge of the other's residence."

I open my mouth to inform him I've no time for supper, but before I can, he takes off his hat and I find myself entranced by the impossible gold of his hair. I have never seen such hair in my life. It's like the sunshine of my childhood is concentrated there.

A door opens beside us, and his hand once again presses against my back. My feet trip forward of their own accord— *traitor feet, what's happening?*—and suddenly we're sitting in a warmly lit booth in a restaurant that smells of garlic and spice. My stomach and heart react at the same time: one with famished hunger and the other with renewed longing for home.

"I thought this would do nicely," he says, and his smile reminds me of the expression my mother's cat, Tubbins, would get when he'd done something particularly clever. "Why did you travel from Melei to attend school?"

"I never said I was a student. And how do you know where I'm from?"

"The beguiling way your mouth forms *S* and *O* gives away your island home."

I raise an eyebrow at his attempt to be clever. "It wasn't my dark skin and black hair?"

He laughs. "Well, those were rather large clues as well. As for the school, see—" He reaches across the table and takes my right hand in his. I try to pull it back, but his long fingers are insistent. "Look at your callus." He points to the raised bump on the top knuckle of my middle finger. "And see how it is stained black? If you were a secretary, no doubt they'd have you on one of those horrible new typewriters. You don't have the pinched look of someone who keeps ledgers, either. And, much like your skin, your school uniform is a bit of a giveaway."

I stifle a snort of laughter, not wanting to give him that point. Then, realizing he still has my hand in his, I pull it back and take a sip of tea. When did the tea get here? Have I been so distracted by his hair? I am not that shallow, surely. But I use the tea to buy myself a moment to look at him. "And what am I studying?"

He taps his chin thoughtfully. "In your final year of preparatory, yes? So you'd have to be in your focus. You have the soulful eyes of a writer and the heavy bag of a reader. Literature, certainly."

"History."

He narrows his eyes. "But that is not your first choice."

"Alas, apparently the feminine mind is not suited to the mathematical arts, all my test scores to the contrary. Now you, sir. Or is it 'lord'?"

"You may address me as anything you wish."

"Well then. You have all the grace and manners of nobility,

not to mention clothes that cost more than our server's yearly wages. Your quick smile indicates an arrogance born and bred into you through generations of never having to answer to anyone, so I'm guessing lord, or perhaps earl, but lord suits your savior complex better. In your spare time, because being wealthy and privileged is a full-time occupation, you like mingling with those too far beneath you for notice. Chambermaids, waitresses," I glance meaningfully at where our serving girl is leaning against the counter gazing moons at him, "and even the occasional student. Unfortunately, sometimes you miscalculate your appeal and try to use your charms on girls who grew up on an island spotted with bastard children who were fathered by visiting Albens. I am therefore immune to being overwhelmed by your exceptional ancestry. You will, however, be able to console yourself with your vast lands and holdings and never again have to consider the student who paid for her own tea and then begged leave."

I dig out my purse and drop a few coins on the table, expecting him to sneer or curse, but instead I look up to find his first genuinely delighted smile. It makes him look younger and I realize he's probably not much older than me. Eighteen, perhaps.

"Oh, please stay and eat, won't you?" he asks. "I haven't had someone be so honest with me in ages, and I cannot tell you how refreshing it is."

Something in the open happiness of his face, the almost childlike hope there, whisks away my resolve to be cold.

"Very well." I sit back and consider my strange companion.

"Though you haven't told me whether or not I'm right, my lord."

"I've no doubt you're right with startling frequency, and while I'd very much like to be yours, I am not a lord. Sandwiches to start?"

The meal is the best I've had since I left Melei. Halfway through, I'm struck with sudden fear for the cost of such a meal, but in one of those odd, sliding moments where I seem to be entranced by the light playing on his hair, the plates are gone and the bill is paid.

"Thank you," I stutter, unsure what else to say. I am out of sorts; I know we've spoken of many things, but I cannot grasp the particulars of any of it.

"Thank *you*, my dear Jessamin. Are you quite sure I can't walk you back to the dormitories?"

I stop midway to standing. "I told you my name?"

His sly smile is back, all innocence gone. "I plucked it from the air around your lips. And for the privilege of knowing it, I'll tell you that mine is Finn."

"Well then, Finn, I wish you the best of luck in your future endeavors, whatever they may be. I do not live in the dormitories, nor do I care to tell you any other details." I scamper from the restaurant. He follows, slower, and I turn to see him over my shoulder, watching me. When I round a corner toward the hotel, I check again to see if he is following, unsure if the thought makes me feel safer or scared.

A large black bird caws over my head, nearly startling me out of my boots. Frowning at it, I unlock the servants' entrance to the Grande Sylvie. Checking over my shoulder one last time, I notice a movement and jump backward.

I shake my head at my nerves. Only my shadow cast by the dim gas lamp.

But for the oddest moment it looked as though I had two.

A TALE OF ROMANCE AND MAGIC

Jessamin has been an outcast since she moved to the dreary country of Albion. Everything changes when she meets Finn, a young lord who introduces her to the secret world of Albion's nobility, a world that has everything Jessamin doesn't—power, money, status . . . and magic.

But Finn is in danger—and it may be up to Jessamin, armed only with her wits and her determination, to save him.

DON'T MISS A SINGLE PAGE OF THE *NEW YORK TIMES* BESTSELLING PARANORMALCY TRILOGY!

NEW YORK TIMES BESTSELLER

PARANORMALCY
KIERSTEN WHITE

SUPERNATURALLY
KIERSTEN WHITE

ENDLESSLY
KIERSTEN WHITE